Violets in the Grass

Jessica (Arael) Marrocco

Edited by Catherine Zembruski

ISBN: 978-1-4525-6029-8 (sc)
ISBN: 978-1-4525-6030-4 (e)

Balboa Press books may be ordered through booksellers or by contacting:

Balboa Press
A Division of Hay House
1663 Liberty Drive
Bloomington, IN 47403
www.balboapress.com
1-(877) 407-4847

Printed in the United States of America

Balboa Press rev. date: 10/16/2012

Contents

Dedication

To my son Rosario, who has added much joy and happiness to my life. He has been my friend and inspiration since his youth.

To my mother, Alba Salvucci Marrocco who always believed in me and supported and encouraged my creative ideas and expressions.

To God and the many wonders of the Universe that inspired these visions and conquests of the other dimensional realms of being.

To my editor, Catherine Zembruski, a retired school teacher, who tirelessly edited this book so I could submit it in a timely nature. Her wonderful assistance and encouragement inspired me to continue to write and share my stories with others. It is her kindness and generosity that helped make this book a reality and I am eternally grateful.

To Mark Jannell, a true friend who has always supported my work and promoted my writings to others. I'm grateful for his encouraging words and feedback about ideas, insights and unbelievable visions.

To James Sheehan, a true Irishman and regressionist, who guided me through my regression into the land of the Fae along with Magda, a wonderful woman who took notes during my regression.

To Stacia St. John and her sister, Robyn John, for allowing me to share their regressions with others. They are both a joy and have much creativity to share with the world.

To my meditation journey class at New Life Endeavors, who have been supportive and an inspiration to my writings. I am blessed to have all of you in my life...Harlyene, Roxanne, Denise, Jose, Carl, Lynn, Stacia, Mark, Ellen, Carolyn, Maureen, Noreen and Craig, and the occasional visitors who float in and out of our lives.

To my group of wonderful friends from Roberta Gray's circle and the inspiration of their works. The trip to Province town with Roberta, John, Deborah and Don, and others helped me see the unity of all things.

To my inner circle of friends who are delighted with my stories and celebrate with me each time something is accomplished. Deborah Nightingale, Pat Volonino, Catherine Zembruski and Kunic Hakaj. Thanks for the cupcake celebrations and the many words of positive feedback and support.

Chapter One

A Regression Into The Past

Regressionist: You are beginning to relax now as the worries and cares of the day are lifting from your shoulders; your mind has a sense of relaxation that begins to fill your body...

The regressionist stands behind me speaking in a soft comforting voice with the gentle music of stringed instruments, sounds of water flowing and birds singing harmoniously together. My body begins to relax and I feel myself sinking deeper into the couch of his office. Despite my logical surroundings I begin to see and feel the garden that he introduces me to during the early part of the regression. A wonderful black scrolling gate that opens up to a flowing brook with trees and large rocks with wild flowers peppered throughout the area in small patches. I see a row of brilliant steps on a mossy green path leading my way into this mystical forest. The music and his voice seem to fade gently into the background and I am engaged with the water and the filtering sun that bathes my cheek gently with the suns nourishing rays. I take a deep breath in and the air smells clean as the freshly watered earth from an afternoon shower. Drops of rain still fixed upon the trees and plants reflect the golden sun rays. The forest becomes illuminated in a sparkling glow of diamonds of green emerald earth. Just as I am floating deeper into this reality I am pulled back by the regressionist's voice.

Regressionist: We are now moving into the past. You will come to a place where you need to understand something about yourself. You are going to enter a place and time where you will see something in your childhood that you need to see.

"Immediately the scene shifted and I was in my youth at Alice's house, the house next door. I was playing with a girl friend in the back yard. We had wandered over to our neighbor's yard because of the lure of something I found quite beautiful. I could feel the spring air blow gently against my hair and face. The noise of my pink windbreaker made the crisp sound of a kite in flight. My eyes were transfixed upon the green grass and the brilliantly blue-purple colors of violets. It was a sea of violets sprinkled through a vibrantly green lawn with spots of bright yellow dandelion flowers and wild weeds of the natural New England landscape. I took in a deep breath as if soaking in the fragrant colors of the earth. I am out of my body observing my youthful wonderment in a moment transfixed with natures magic. I reach toward the grass to pluck up the violets in a miniature bouquet perfectly suited for a child of six or seven years of age. My hand goes deeper into the tall grass and an unusual mist begins to pour in. I can still see the flowers and the grass but the mist has altered the depth of field. A portal appears and the grass seems to reveal a landscape from beyond.

An unusual unseen force pulls me through like a magnet and I am drawn into this window or portal to the other dimensional worlds. Within a flash of bright light my body becomes still. I reach to touch my own chest near my heart. I look down and observe the clothing I am wearing. It all appears to be the same as before, yet I feel very different. A part of me is gone, the part of innocence of a child as I am feeling somewhat impish or daring. A smirking grin of a rebellious nature, yet mischief now enters my thoughts like never before. I want to prank and challenge the neighbor whose land I am now exploring. I no longer feel fear or apprehension. The realm I had entered was the netherworld, the land of the Fae. It was I who had been turned into a changeling, a fairy of sorts, a seer of other dimensions, a child of the Fae as my other life diminished in some type of way. I lift as if I could float and have wings. My eyes are now focused on many magical things and I peer into the sun rays announcing that I had made my entrance through the magical mystic misty haze. I am now free and now complete. My soul no longer needs to retreat. I float as a butterfly and sing about with freedom from the world that I came from...Shift the circle of my breath and make me feel the thoughts of what is best. I encounter freedom from the open door and now the portal has closed once more. I am free as the bees in the summer sun. I fly in my soul to explore all that has come and I know that many will know my name as I was sent before to help the earth heal again.

I think to myself, "Who is this speaking so bold and assertive unlike my former self."Is that me? What has happened? An attached spirit? I try to shake it from me but to no avail. It doesn't move. It is connected to me like my shadow. A part of me that has reconnected. A piece of my soul that was lost and re-joined when the opportunity did arise. I try to shake it once again from me but to no avail. It is me. How could this be? It had taken on a new personality, or so I thought was the truth. Then I began to contemplate the many things that made me waiver in this idea. The expressions I was now seeing was going on the inside of me all the time. The energy of freedom and a release from fear had now taken on the form of a winged creature quite often referred to as a fairy. A fairy, how ridiculous! What absurdity to imagine that I had formerly been a fairy. I mocked my own vision and suggested that I was probably the tooth fairy here to support the well-being of youthful dental hygiene.

Stop! I pause again. What just happened, none-the-less, must be addressed. Why am I rhyming?...I pause again. This is foolish. I am so full of fantasy this time that I can't get out. I must face the fact that something changed that day. Is there any other explanation for this. Still in a daze I observe this ongoing conversation in my mind. Yet I have been revived to something new. Despite my internal mental resistance I feel wonderful, I feel light and complete as a soul. I feel an inner strength that I never experienced before and fearless like no other time. The vision began to swirl away as the regressionist called me forward once again to return back in time another six or seven years and remember when I entered my mother's womb. He directed me to observe what happened before I was born.

Regressionist: Where are you now?

Arael: "I'm in my neighbor's back yard picking violets and there is a mist in the grass." I could feel my face grin with serenity.

Regressionist: Almost like the mists of Avalon...?

I paused, not quite sure what this meant but it jumped out in a way that stirred a deeper part of my memory. He proceeded to ask another question seeing that I could not respond to his words.

Regressionist: Who is there with you?

Arael: A neighborhood friend.

Regressionist: Is she seeing what you are seeing?

Arael: No, she is too worried about getting yelled at by our neighbor.

Regressionist: What are you doing now?

Arael: She calls my name and wants to leave because I am dancing around the grass and drawing too much attention to us in the back yard. I am fearless but she is worried.

A quiet pause...as the music plays faintly in the background. He takes in a deep breath and continues with the regression.

Regressionist: We are now going to move back further into the past, we're moving back further into the past now all the way to before you were born and in your mother's womb.

Regressionist: Do you see yourself in your mother's womb

Arael: Yes

Regressionist: What is going on in your mother's mind right now and how does she feel about you being born?

Arael: She is caught up with the many distractions of my older brothers and sister.

Regressionist: Oh, you have brothers and sisters there. What is happening with her and your brothers and sister and what is she feeling?

Arael: I can feel their energy running around the house and distracting her from thinking about me or anything else, for that matter.

Regressionist: Do you feel that it is bad that she is not thinking of you or not very excited about having another child?

Arael: No, I feel that she loves my brothers and sister and is overwhelmed at times by their energy. She doesn't think about me because I am not on the outside yet.

Regressionist: Are you saying that she still sees you as herself and, at this time, with other children to care for, she doesn't have much time for herself?

Arael: Yes, that is what I am saying. I don't feel bad that she is not thinking about me. She is so distracted by their high energy so much that she doesn't have a moment to think about me, as I am still connected to her.

"I didn't express this to him but I felt that I could think and feel as she did. This was something that happened throughout my life time with her and our personalities were very similar in some ways while I was growing up and there was always an inner understanding that was never spoken. The time in our mother's womb becomes such a transformational time that we rarely recognize the environment that formulates our very entrance into the earthly plane.

Regressionist: It is now time for you to enter the world and be born. Can you see yourself being born.

Arael: I am having trouble seeing. The light is so bright. The light is much too bright and I can't see anything. However, I feel free from my mother's constant worries and concerns and feel a liberation of my empathic soul.

"He continues to speak but it is too far in the background and I can barely hear his voice. The entrance into the world from my mother's womb was too strong. I don't sense any pain but rather disorientation and an extraordinarily bright light that seems to startle my senses. I can't see beyond this and then his voice begins to get louder.

Regressionist: On the count of ten you are now returning back and becoming more alert and aware of your surroundings. You are starting to hear the sounds around the room and are returning to the present life time now. You are now wide awake...

I open my eyes and continue to have the feelings of waking up from a very surreal dream. My eyes become transfixed on the ceiling and walls of the office to help myself reorient my thoughts to the surroundings of where I am at. His voice is much louder and I am back into my consciousness of being."

Regressionist: How was this experience for you?

Arael: It was wonderful almost as if I was in a very mystical place with mists in the forest.

Regressionist: It sounded like you had a pleasant childhood.

Arael: I suppose it had it's challenges but I did feel love from my mother and there were points of joy and happiness of being a child. I'm glad I had that experience to remind me of that. "The session ended and I had to ponder what happened during this time. It wasn't until two years later that I was able to listen to this regression. I think I wasn't able to process the unusual happenings that occurred that clearly brought me to a point in my life where I may have stepped into the other dimensional realms that may have changed my very existence in some way. This was all quite fascinating to me and had me believing that my early transformation contributed to my memory of being able to see inter-dimensionally at times, not recognizing early on that not everyone was experiencing this reality as I did. Yet, I grew to discover that their were others around me who had similar experiences with other realms of reality and they reminded me of what I am and who I became. These other like-minded people may have also stepped through the veils of reality to capture a piece of their etheric souls as I did; and they could confirm some of my understanding of how a person could walk between the realms of two worlds or alternate realities."

Chapter Two

The Visitors

AFTER THE REGRESSION I BEGAN TO LOOK into the darker shadows of my childhood. There was an eeriness about my childhood home. Some friends of the family claimed that it was haunted, as they would reveal some odd experience or encounter some paranormal behavior during a time while they were in the basement. I tended to agree with them because I had an acute sensitivity to the paranormal in my youth and felt very attuned to the darkness that overtook the image of my home in a faint memory of shadows.

Yes, it was shadows of things not seen. I can recall that after opening this portal of sorts, I began entering another part of my life that was so much less joyful. Still only six or seven years in age, it all began with a lucid dream one night. I felt as if I was somehow transported to the outside of my home. The stars were bright and they contrasted with the evening sky with a sparkle that I had not seen before. There I was, standing in front of my home and gazing upward, fully dressed in my usual clothing. My thoughts were filled with questions regarding how I got outside and where were my parents and other siblings. There, hovering over my home, was a saucer-like space craft that seemed so large and obvious. It was just floating there, soundless and moving slightly horizontally in a gentle flow. It moved back and forth to help stabilize the motion, then slightly vertical upward and down to show the reality of it's existence. The most striking part of this scene was the visual distortion of my neighborhood. It almost appeared as if we were at the top of the Earth, all else was beneath and curved downward. The houses seemed to curve as if I were viewing it all from a fish-eyed lens. I was awestruck...Then the dream ended and I awoke from this vision and was back in my bedroom looking out the window and saw that everything had returned back to normal. I fell back to sleep and awoke with a strange memory of what may have happened.

Then the nightmares began. Every night I was aware of a presence so powerful and military-like that I felt the emotion of sheer horror. I was terrified by the dreams that the Robots were coming or that they were already here. I never saw them at that time but the impression I got is that they were small but methodical in their approach. They didn't feel human. They seemed insensitive to human emotion. They were on a mission to take over or take something that they needed. For some reason, I became one of their contacts. Little did I know that it was because I energetically opened up into another dimensional realm that opened the door for other dimensional beings to step in. None of this was comprehensible to me at the time since I was so young. It took so many years later for me to realize that they were merely trying to stop the influx of other problems that were seeping into our time lines and altering our reality, moreover, altering the reality of the future.

What exactly did the future hold for us? It was unclear. Yet, I often wonder if my first spiritual experience may have set things into motion that were not necessarily bad. Time would tell and years later I am still searching for these answers.

It may appear that the Robots no longer were angry at me and the nightmares had ended. I returned back to my seemingly normal childhood with a curiosity for the supernatural.

My daydreaming continued and I became enamored by the outdoors and played fervently in my neighborhood and local parks. I did endless cartwheels, flips, backbends, jump roping, and jungle-gym climbing. I was very much like the average child who burned off energy from dawn until dusk and then went back home to have dinner after hearing my mother's voice calling me home. I watched the sun set in brilliant pink-peach blue skies of summer dreams. I played with buttercups like the other neighborhood children by holding a flower under my chin to see if I really liked or didn't like something. If I liked something the buttercup would make the underneath side of my chin turn yellow. The games were as simple as hide and seek and Chinese jump rope. I had a bike and a pogo stick to jump on and a hula hoop to whirl. I played paddy cake, Mary Mack and other games like jacks. Hours would go by and when I came home the house was still full of people with five brothers and sisters and parents. The neighborhood was close and we never had to travel far to play.

One day while I was doing handstands on the front lawn with friends I noticed something strange. I could see weird patterns and circular bubble-like structures in the air. I reached out in front of me to see if it was solid. My hand moved carefully forward to touch the patterns or pop the bubbles that I was seeing while my friends watched me wave my hands.

Arael: " Do you see that?"

Friend: "See what? What are you talking about and why are you waving your hand as if there is something in front of you?

I stood there for a moment and tried to move from other angles still observing this strange phenomenon. I also had a strange sensation as if I was being monitored, listened to and watched. It was not to the degree of paranoia or fear, it was very matter-of-fact. They were observing me and I was getting accustomed to it since there was nothing I could do to prevent it.

Arael: "You really can't see the air the way I see it? It looks like it has some type of bubbles."

More children began gathering around to see what I was looking at and couldn't see anything. They never laughed at me because they knew that my honesty was a distinct characteristic of my personality. Still, they were troubled that I was seeing something and I never mentioned it again. Similar to my nightmares, I continued seeing this strange phenomenon in the air while I played outside. This happened particularly on my front lawn and I decided to accept the fact that no one else could see what I was seeing. Eventually, like the nightmares, they faded to black, and remained in my memory as only an archive of strange happenings from my past. I never saw that strange texture in the air again.

I began to grow older and more aware of my surroundings. I no longer got caught up in fairy tales or strange phenomena. I could easily step into my own daydreaming world and fantasize to my hearts desire.

Then the voices began.There was my bedroom closet that seemed to be filled with old women from centuries before trying to haunt me from their New England Witch Trial cells. "You will never be happy. Your life is going to be filled with problems. We can see you from everywhere." I didn't like these women because they never said a word of kindness. Hiding in the depths of their own personal hell and caught between worlds. Bitter to the end, they had a venom for me that wreaked of burning flesh.

Arael: "Why do you hate me? I don't even know who you are. You should go back to where you came from. I never did anything to you."

Old Woman: "You accused us of doing wicked deeds in the darkness of night. You sent us to the gallows."

Arael: "It wasn't me, I can assure you that you have confused me with someone else."

The voices became quiet as I held my ground and they finally became convinced of my innocence and tormented me no more.

Sure enough, they found in me, someone who would hear and listen to their bitter torment. They had been cruelly judged by the Puritanical rule of New England in the 1600's during the Salem Witch trials. What a nightmare that never ended for them. Yet, why punish me? I was a young child who may have looked similar to their accusers, however it wasn't me and they had to accept their error. They also disappeared in time and undoubtedly found other victims to frighten. Similar to the Robots, I could sense their presence and hear them. My sight of them was limited as I could only see them in shadows. Years later, I came to understand that they were caught in this reality and were seeking help out of there. At that time in my life I was not able to help them into the light.

A quietness set in as I entered the eighth year of my life. Now seemingly clear of all monsters and wicked spirits, I was coming into my youth exploring the natural world, expanding my mind through books and music. I could recall another incident when an unexplained event happened in my home....

I was in my den seated on the carpet by a record player exploring the many sounds of music that my older siblings were listening to: the sounds of Crosby, Stills & Nash, Jethro Tull, Gordon Lightfoot or Steppenwolf's Magic Carpet Ride. These were not your average pop stars of pre-teens at the time. I also remember listening to a few songs of the Beatles. I'm not exactly sure, what I was listening to when an unexpected visitor stepped into the den.

Woman: Hello, do you remember me?

I was relaxed and sitting on the carpet when she arrived and instantly jumped up from where I sat, being startled by her abrupt entrance. Her entire behavior was highly aggressive and demanding of me.

Arael: No, I don't remember you. Who did you come to visit?

I got up from the floor and sat on a couch in the room and looked at her eyes. There was something wrong with her eyes as they didn't appear natural. They were very blue and attractive but not kind and she almost had a hostile look, although the tone of her voice was very friendly. Her hair was brown and above the shoulder length with slight waves to it. Her skin was fair and not typical of my usual relatives who had Italian olive skin. She was tall and thin and dressed as if she was going to work not on a visit to a friend's house. Everything was wrong...and yet I couldn't figure out exactly how to identify this problem.

Woman: I came to visit you. Can I hold your hand?

I pulled my hand back and refused to let her touch me. She realized that I didn't trust her and she left the room. I waited a while and then walked over to the kitchen to see if my mother was entertaining her. She was nowhere in sight. I then spoke to my mother...

Arael: Where did that woman go? Is she a friend of yours?

Mother: What woman?

Arael: The strange woman who came into the den who was just talking to me.

"Then I went on to describe her appearance and what she said."

Mother: "Oh, stop your foolishness Arael! No one has been in our house during the past few hours except for the two of us."

It happened again...I walked back to the den and began looking around. I looked out the front window to see if there was a car parked outside. Come to think of it, I never heard a door open or close. This was a mystery that I carried throughout my life. It is one thing to see a spirit in another dimension. The rest of the natural surroundings remain in view and the spirit takes on an etheric form. In this happening, the woman was in human form. I will never know what her hand felt like and I may never know what could have happened to me had I touched her hand. Maybe I would have been missing...I'm not sure. Maybe, it just would have been a handshake and she would have left satisfied that I accepted her presence. One never knows the outcome. Similar to the mist in the violets and grass, I could have changed somehow but still remained on this Earthly plain. Later in my life I came to understand that extraterrestrial beings can come to visit and appear as human. This made more sense to me because she didn't seem to be a person who was dead or stuck between the dimensions with all the confusion that may carry. Instead, this being didn't have the normal energy of a human soul, rather it's energy was quite powerful, direct and intimidating. I knew there was a higher knowledge beyond our human capacity. It turned out that later I discovered that she was, in fact, an extraterrestrial male being with similar eyes, who was very tall and had a bulbous shaped head, and wore a long robe. The interaction with this being was one of the many tests that I would experience throughout my life. I was to remember, though incarnated with a loss of much of my soul memory of past lives and instruction, that I should not trust the beings who were to enter into my life as they could be dangerous to me and my well-being. Ultimately, I passed the test and was able to proceed on my journey of many other types of tests that helped to raise me back up to a place of remembrance of why I am here and what my life's purpose is. Much of this comes later and this lesson was a step up a set of stairs that seemed to go on into oblivion. The challenges were set before me and it was a slight time of awakening that stirred my soul into seeing that each step would be momentous as well as victorious. Years later I recall looking at an album of Boston in that same den and having the sinking feeling and memory of my surreal dream of a very similar looking space ship that hovered over my house and the memory of the visiting woman who no one else could see. I could hear in the background the song of Steppenwolf's Jupiter's Child came in loud and clear.

The most prominent memory of a visitation was the one I call, "The Romans." They could have been my relatives but they weren't. If there is such a thing as the Roman Gods, I believe this was them. At a very young age I remember meeting with them in my parent's bedroom. The strange part was that the bed was gone and the room was rearranged. I talked to a strong man who treated me like a long lost relative. He called me forward and picked me up gently and very lovingly. I remember I didn't want him to go. There were others around and they picked me up and held me as well. I was five or six years old at that time.

Arael: What are you doing in my parent's room and why are you here?

Roman: We came to visit you and make sure you are well.

Then he reached down and picked up Arael and held her in his arms. His eyes were kind and gentle and wet with tears.

Roman: We've been worried about you and what you have been going through. We tried to help you but he wouldn't allow us.

Arael: Who doesn't want you to help me?

Roman: Our Father, he said you need to learn more before we can help you.

Arael: He doesn't like me does he?

Roman: No, he is very strict with his rules and he said you need to learn more.

Arael: Am I bad? Have I done something wrong?

Roman: You need to learn more before you can return home. There will be many more experiences in your life before you can come back to us. We want to rescue you out of this place but we are not able to without his permission.

His eyes filled with tears again.

Roman: You will have a hard time and many sorrows along the way.

He held her with one arm and brushed her hair from her face and then continued speaking:

Roman: You have work to do here and when it is finished he will come to you. When he is happy with you he will arrive and speak with you about your work. Don't feel frightened. We'll be watching over you but we cannot interfere. You must make the right decisions and stay on the path he has given you even if it is painful at times. I will tell you many things but you will not remember most of it until much later in time.

He never gave me his name but I will never forget his crystal blue eyes, round face, black curly hair and a slightly scruffy unshaven face. He was large in stature and muscular but cherubic as well. Later in time I came to equate him with Bacchus the Roman god of wine and... Years later I would see him in a vision in a place that is called the Pleiades...The seven sister stars. There he sat in a room full of beautiful pillars and marble floors while he laid comfortably on plush pillows. It was Bacchus, and once again I was a child in his arms. He, in both occasions, appeared to be a caretaker of me in my youth in other dimensions, times and places. I believe the place was Olympus or the place of the Gods as mentioned in the old Greek and Roman myths. I remembered all of this as I grew older and my vision of the Pleiades stars made me convinced that this had to be a dimension of reality that was more engaged in the human experience at one time.

Time had passed and a few years had gone by as the seasons had changed and I grew older and more aware of my surroundings. My youth escorted me into pre-pubescence.

My grandmother came to stay with us. Her hair was as black as a raven at one time. Now, she was frail from old age and was challenged with the struggles of cancerous cells invading her body. I moved out of my bedroom so she could have a place to rest in her final days. She was from a true Gypsy stock. One could tell by her green eyes and dark olive skin that she came from a lineage of exotic seers. She never said anything about intuition, psychic abilities, palm reading or tea leaves. Yet, it was her decision for my sister to inherit the Italian name for gypsy, "Zingara." I was never quite sure about the spelling but when she looked past me with my fairer skin tone, blue eyes and golden brown hair, I knew she had made a mistake! She never knew that I was a seer. I never told her that but she assumed that it was someone else who carried the gift. Still she ignored me, looking past me as if I wasn't in the room. I never said much to her because I knew that we didn't have a bond. Still, my room was hers and we kindly visited her with treats of rainbow sherbet to ease her cancerous pain. In solitude and contemplation I saw her spirit grow weak with age and illness until she quietly passed as she slept. I was not upset with her but rather disconnected. What did I need to learn here? Not everyone connects to one another as we are different and carry preferences, likes and dislikes in the people we are attracted to. My grandfather, her husband, who died many years before, was very much a jolly soul and his pure white hair and blue eyes were always full of laughter. I had this memory to take with me and enjoy.

All along there was much turmoil in my home from teenage rebellion amongst my much older siblings. They would struggle with my parent's rules and became lawless with the time and the 60's hippy movement that was so prevalent. My brothers wouldn't cut their hair, my sister would find a boyfriend who was too old for her. The victory of athleticism in all of them grew cold. None carried the flame of enthusiasm for a worthy cause. Yet, they were 'East Coast Groovy' and really into the hippy scene. My oldest brother went to Woodstock. Peer pressure was very powerful and much of the athletic talent was wasted on verbal battles of parental frustration. The oldest went off to college, acquiring a degree. The other two got married young. Now in my house was left only three. Three siblings to deal with war torn parents of a hard generational challenge. We would visit my second oldest brother's hippy pad that had psychedelic pictures on the wall, hanging beads in the doorways, exotic looking pillows on the floor and an endless list of girlfriends. This brother also had an amazing talent in art. He could draw anything and, like my mother, he had a seriousness about his work. I also had the gift to draw and a fascination with color that I would continue to explore much later in my life. So many images of mushrooms, flowers, peace signs, clothing and the earthiness, tolerance and other wonderful qualities of the hippy movement came to the forefront for me. I was much too young to understand the psychedelic drugs but I did like the imagery, the other-dimensional realities that seem to become more acceptable now. I could feel a little more free to express myself as this became intertwined within our culture. The vividness of color was from the surreal world of my daydreaming and lucid dreams. They matched my other dimensional realities that confirmed my experiences that didn't set me apart as being the only one who viewed as an observer in a space where matter could move, bend and wave. This was also a place where time could stand still or shift into alternate realities.

Innocence was lost for many during that period in time. I often felt immobilized by the household turmoil that seemed to flourish like a heavy weed in a wildflower garden. It was loud and boisterous with anger and frustration. There was no hope on the horizon as discord continued to rise. Here were three fiery teenagers searching for personal independence and freedom of expression in one of the most difficult and challenging times of our nation's history. It was an end of an era and the awakening of souls had begun...but not without a price. There was deep discord throughout the nation as parents heartbreakingly watched their children drift off aimlessly as if an invisible pied piper was calling them off to work. I empathically felt the pain of it all. Just to make matters more confusing, many were using experimental drugs that were easily obtained on the streets. This entire generation was used as guinea pigs in a massive laboratory of insensitivity to the human soul. Many were lost in this binge of confusion. Many had spiritual experiences that they could have had without the poisonous chemicals. Many continue to live in a vial of confusion. The cursed beast had plunged it's poison into the mix of humanity and taken many souls into the darkness of night. The healing continues until this day. I was an observer who searched for answers as a child and tried to sort through the confusion of the time and the impact it had on my personal home life. These were only the beginning of the pains that I had to endure.

Not experiencing any strange paranormal behavior for a while I thought that much of my strange memories were merely childhood whims. At this time I thought that I was fully grounded into the natural time-space-reality of the human experience. I was soon reminded once again that the other dimensional door around me could still allow visitors to come in.

I then had another unexplained visitation at my home. I can recall standing by the threshold between the living room and dining room when two men appeared who looked like pixies but human in size and scale. Their entrance came through with a popping sound of magic. Their hair was black but their upturned noses and mischief in their eyes seems to imply that they were the elementals of the earth, similar to when I stepped into the realm of the Fae while I was a child playing in the grass and picking violets. Like a flash of light they appeared before me. They said, "There she is! We found her!" Instantly, they disappeared in front of my eyes before I could ask, "There who is? or Who are you?" It was too late, they were gone. What is happening around here and why is no one else around when this happens? Troubled by this vision I had a pit in my stomach and felt all knotted up inside. "What is going to happen to me next? This was not going to be good!"

I went to my bedroom and could hear verbal taunts from the other dimensional realm challenging and threatening to cause me trouble. "What was this all about? Apparently I had ticked someone off and they were set on being vengeful against me. I claimed my innocence of course. This was not only confusing but I could not remember who they were in the first place. The verbal contention continued and they said I would have to pay for what had happened. I thought to myself, "I don't believe this! Even Peter Pan hates me now!" After a bit of a discussion I finally got them to calm down. The Fae are quite mischievous and can be reasoned with if you have the patience. Still, they were never quite clear about why they were angry at me. A bit of miscommunication, a flutter fit of frustration, they talked so quickly that I hardly got a word in edgewise.

Arael: LISTEN! I don't know what you are talking about. Is it possible that you have me confused with someone else?

Then I heard a voice in a munchkin sort of tone,

Pixie: It could be that we had mistaken you for someone else, but just to make sure, we will give you a bit of your own medicine.

I thought, Great...now what does that mean. Here they are threatening me and I don't have the faintest idea about what they are talking about and who the others were who probably pinned it on me. I couldn't even imagine how I got in this mess but I knew they were angry. I know we laugh and mock at the thought of fairy's, pixies, gnomes, elves, trolls, and the like...but they are vengeful folk if they are crossed or mocked in a way. It seems that they don't like to be disrespected and are conscious of their status, size and assumed weakness in most matters. On the other hand it is quite contrary, they have a form of magical power that can carry a curse that reaches back to the Emerald Isle where they come from. Though we cannot see them physically, they have a responsibility to care for the earth and they demand our respect. I know I sound like an old Irish storyteller on this topic but let the wise heed my warning.

They live on the earth or in the subterranean realm of the earth hidden by a veil of mystery like the mist. They hide from the human eye that allows only a few to see into this realm, with the exception to those who have the gift of second sight, as the old Scottish Mystic, Robert Kirk, from *The Secret Commonwealth* said. Not all can peer into this dimension unless your heart is pure, you respect the green earth and you are able to see as a child. If this is true, then I have never grown up and that Peter Pan was in for a battle!

Arael: Who are you and why are you accusing me of doing things I haven't done!

My voice became bold and much more assertive as I stood my ground and my memory of who these little people were.

The pixie became silent and listened.

Pixie: Do you remember us?

Arael: Well of course I do (in reality I didn't have a clue but I held my ground)

Pixie: We were told that you stole something sacred from our grounds when you entered in the realm as a little girl.

Arael: This is preposterous! Of course not! If you can recall, I returned to my home empty-handed.

Pixie: We have a record of this you know and we are able to observe whether or not you betrayed our kingdom.

The movie was reviewed by them and sure enough it was true. I was innocent.

Pixie: My apologies my fairest one. However, we were told by the Wise Ones that you would help us get our sacred stone back for us.

Arael: I will find it now for you if you direct me to the right place or person.

Pixie: No, it is well hidden by magic and the deceivers had left our garden the same time you entered. You opened the doorway to our realm and the rebellious ones escaped. We thought you were there to help them.

Arael: I entered your realm by accident. I was merely picking violets in the grass when a magical mist appeared. Before I knew it I was being sucked back into your realm and something attached to me as if a soul piece joined my soul and made me more complete.

Pixie: Oh...so you were sent by the higher realms? Is that so?

He commented sarcastically.

Pixie: We shall see the test of time if you are who you claim to be. For no one is allowed to enter our realm uninvited unless they have the higher realm's gifts and abilities. So, you had learned from King Arthur. Are you the dark one from the lake or do you have the light of Guinevere? Time will tell... I see both good and bad within you now. Much of your darkness will be sifted out so we can see if you have favor with the Fae. If not, there is much to amend for your wicked ways. Begone now and search for those robbers for whom we will hold you responsible.

A feeling of dread came over me. I knew this feeling from before and it wouldn't be until much later in my life that I would discover my connection to the Fae and how they required me to assist in locating and returning the sacred stone that they had been searching for. I don't doubt that the spiritual imbalance of this incident had manifested into other problems on our earth. I had made a commitment to resolve this problem even though I had stumbled upon it accidentally. I can't help but think that this was part of the destiny of my childhood. The angels hovered over me so I would keep my word and stay the course in a less inviting journey moving forward. I longed for an easier path but I knew somehow that it would be better to just stay the course despite the challenges and burdens I needed to bare. Nearly 40 years would pass before that stone would be returned.

Life continued on in a somewhat normal fashion. I was in school, learning and on my free time I was spending time with neighborhood friends. The days grew longer as young adulthood started to set in and I was beginning to put away the things of my childhood. It was somewhat of a paradox, I was getting older, more mature than many my age, yet, I felt youthful and playful when the spirit moved me to express my mischievous sprite inside. My mind took me to the darkest of places where witches and goblins hid and then within a flash of a moment I was off like an acrobat flipping and spinning on the grass, jumping and doing acrobatics like a whimsical fairy, swirling around, light and silly...the elf-like gestures of a practical joker and singing foolish songs or running with all my might to climb the highest backstop on the Baseball field. Fearless, energetic in nature, I claimed my right to be named amongst the Fae. Strong, sensible and mature, I displayed the more serious part of my human life. I carried on and began to see things a little differently. My body was changing as I began to enter puberty. My eyes began to drift toward boys and within my circle of friends we planned our first kiss. We didn't dare try to do this alone and instead of playing spin the bottle we had already known who should be matched with who.

Quietly we hid behind the grand shrubs in front of the elementary school and after the count of ten the 5 couples had the fastest kiss on the lips that one could ever imagine. I closed my eyes and it was over faster than a snap of a finger. I remember opening my eyes and the boy and I kissed and then smiled with blushing faces. We were very nervous to leave the shrubs right away for fear that we may get caught by an adult. I was in fifth grade but my courage for something like this gave me a sense of uneasiness. The mischief in my life was something that would surprise people at times. For myself, I recognized what fun it could be if everyone had just a little mischief to play with. There is really no reason to be so uptight and restricted, after all, it could be quite boring. Now, I'm not saying that it is good to harm others or do anything that is completely lawless. I'm merely saying that a little mischief never hurt anyone...

Our next step was to enter Middle School. I can't imagine how wonderful that would be to have the aspirations of being more adult and gaining more independence. The gift of knowledge always comes with new challenges, experiences and responsibilities. None of which seemed important to me. I was searching for more adventure and the kiss behind the shrubs was something that I needed to explore some more, particularly if I was to figure out whether or not I really liked to kiss boys. After all, this is a new experience and I needed to try it at least a few more times before I could make this decision.

Unfortunately, that summer I grew like a weed, not unlike Alice in Wonderland. I grew to my full height, an amazing 5'6' which left me towering over a majority of the boys in my class. What happened to me and why am I so large? Or, at least tall, fortunately, I didn't get wider as well. All the people looked little, or were they just little people? I needed to wait a few more years to see if any of them would grow. My transformation was so noticeable that some of my classmates thought I was a substitute teacher from behind. What a foul trick nature had played on me. Anyhow, I had to come to terms with this. It was going to be another challenge to face. It turned out to be a good year, however my romantic curiosity was somewhat placed on a back burner and I enjoyed the fun of being with friends. That awkward feeling never left me completely until after I had graduated from high school.

After my Grandmother died it wasn't long before my father was diagnosed with cancer. It was a strange feeling to see my Father sitting in on the couch saying nothing and being completely listless. My father was usually larger than life and his personality impacted everyone in our family and all who knew us. He was a true Leo, being born during the month of August with a personality that demanded subservience. All of us were to bow to his strict rules and strong words. We didn't dare rebel, for those who did enter that arena tasted a bit of his wrath. A self-proclaimed ruler of his own house, the Leo parent sits above the pack with a roaring thunder. He didn't have to say much, when he entered the room everyone became subdued. He was only 5'8 but many called him "Big Al." Big on personality as we were told, when he walked down the street people would get out of his way because of the level of intimidation they felt around him. The other side of his personality was a quick wit filled with sarcasm. He would sit on the couch with a toothpick hanging out of his mouth. With his dark olive skin, black hair, and sharp dark brown eyes, he could sense anything around him. We couldn't fool him or hide anything. He always knew when something was going on. As I grew older I remembered the stories he told us about his earlier years before we were born. He was raised by a mother who was of Italian descent and educated enough that she was a book keeper or qualified accountant. My grandfather came directly from Italy from town called Fondi, from the region of Abruzzi. Their three children were all musical and would perform as a family band in local churches.

He had an unusual perspective of life that he rarely spoke about. It as almost as if he had a lot of anger that he didn't know how to release or address. Years later I suspected It was his skin color. Despite his obvious European heritage he mentioned times of prejudice against the Italians and other dark-skinned Europeans. The story that stood out to me most was the time when he was in the Navy and on leave in the U.S. He traveled in the South during the 1940's and was pulled over for no apparent reason and thrown into jail. My father was never one to say he was a victim in any circumstance, however, on this occasion there was a look in his eyes of being mistreated without a cause. I wouldn't be surprised if this was his life time frustration, being quite intelligent and very street smart, he stood with a dignified look but acted as if he needed to be strong in a world where men of color or nationality didn't have their place or couldn't achieve above a certain level of status. Italians kept very close to each other and usually worked together because they understood challenges of being an immigrant with less opportunities available to them. All of my ancestors worked with stones in masonry and construction of buildings. They were the builders of this city as well as many other cities as they created sturdy masterpieces of beautiful stonework buildings and had skills that were passed down from the ancient Romans. You might be thinking...why is she going off into this tangent or soap box about her ancestry. This is the place when I grew to understand that all humans were created equally. Not one is above another. The value of one culture is not greater or worse than others. We all came from one source. The God Energy Source. A power that ties each and every one of us together in an unseen grid of energy. If you are being challenged with the issues of prejudice today, you are still working on your own soul's challenge to forgive, accept and become a part of the universal whole.

When I looked at my father I felt as if the old ideas of the past were falling away. I sat next to him and for the first time I could hear him think. He was quiet, filled with pain killing medicine that made him seem very distant. At the age of twelve I knew he was ready to take his journey to the other side. I had a dream that informed me of his death before anyone else mentioned it. I also became aware of the fact that when we cannot change with the consciousness of the time we come to the close of our life purpose. Had we taken another road and became open to the changes and flow of consciousness then our lives could be extended until our Dharma is fulfilled.' I had one very memorable conversation with him before his death. He was seated on his bed and I was by his side.

Father: Sit down next to me and let's talk for a little bit.

He always called me Jasper. I'm not sure why; he never explained things like this. He had nicknames for all of us. Some of my siblings had more than one nickname. My name was consistent. It was always Jasper. The story he told me when I was a child is that he thought I was going to be a boy. That was the reason why he originally called me Jesse. I was supposed to be named after Jesse James. I thought that was amusing since Jesse James was such a notorious bank robber. What could he have been thinking? It was a sense of humor and wit that was so typical of him. It is this type of name that would become a conversation piece, at my expense, of course. He was always ready to tease or embarrass us around others and we became used to it and we'd just shake our heads at his silly comments. I guess it was his way of showing us his love. Another thing that he would do is create competitions amongst us. He would encourage us to race one another or see who could do more sit-ups or push-ups, who could hold the longest in a leg lift. We were in such good condition that my younger sister and I were more physically fit than my brother's friends who were four years older than us. There wasn't a sports team that I couldn't make and my brothers reputation in school athletics preceded us. We were remembered as an athletic family in town and respected for our passion for the game.

After he died I remembered walking past his bedroom one day and feeling his strong stare coming from the room. It was so powerful that I stopped cold in my tracks and peered into the room and tried to understand what just happened. I knew he was there. Yet, I couldn't see him. His presence was so overwhelming that I found it disturbing. I know the journey was not easy for him. He had not resolved all his mistakes and decisions that caused him to avoid the light. Many do this and become earthbound. They are afraid of a judgement that they were not willing to face. They don't realize that there is mercy and forgiveness if they ask for it.

Many years later I was in a meditation group with a few mediums. My father showed up and one of the woman named Barbara asked me if I had any issues with my father.

Barbara: I see someone who I believe was your father but he seems to be hiding from you. Do you know why he feels this way?

Arael: I think he feels ashamed or upset at some of the decisions he made in his life but I am not his judge. I would love to help him go into the light.

I knew what she was talking about. He knew we all had a healthy fear of him and his strict ways. I wasn't angry or upset with him and some of this didn't make any sense. I concentrated and tried to make the connection and could see him hiding behind what appeared to be a pole. I talked to him gently and he came out and I saw him escorted into the light with a few angels. It took over 30 years for this to happen. I'm glad that he is in a place where he should be. There were a few more occasions where I saw him and each time he seemed to be at peace.

With the passing of my father I had a sense of freedom. His strict rules and guidelines were very binding for a free spirit like myself. I had no intention of exploring drugs or alcohol to the degree that others did before me. I had learned that substances were not only dangerous but could destroy a person's life in many ways. That was a hard lesson learned by people much older than I, and so I never really indulged in this behavior. Unfortunately, it was the peak of the 70's and drugs and alcohol were easy to acquire for anyone my age. Some friends and classmates got heavily into drugs and alcohol. Of course, not all of them were into drugs but took in the occasional drink from their parent's bar or sat by a local reservoir and met to have a beer or two with a group of peers. It was a social time, nothing extreme, a lot of talking, flirting and fun. Later on, I saw the wisdom of what I had observed and the decision I made at a very early age was to not do drugs. I realized when I was older that all of my strange communications with many unexplained visitors were not tainted by drugs or alcohol. To this day I stay clear of everything including some of the drugs used for spiritual journeys such as Iawaska and Peyote. I respect that this is a part of the native culture in both the native people of this country and South America. However, one must remember the journey out of the body is one thing, but can the spirit return safely when the depths of reality are skewed by a hallucinogenic substance. One needs a strong spiritual guide to help him/her back into the body; a person that he/she knows and trusts completely. Otherwise, my belief is that many can have this experience without being chemically or herbal induced if they take deeper meditative journeys. That allows a person to control his/her own body and step out if he/she chooses to do so in a much safer way.

The greatest thing that I discovered during the time of the unexplained visitors is that we are all on this journey to self-realization and understanding the depths of our souls between life and death as well as the exploration of the many dimensional realities that exist around us. No one is more special or gifted than another. We all have our own individual purpose. We all come from the Universal God life force as every one of us carries a spark of the Divine.

I watched a movie about a little boy named Hugo, who had a robot given to him by his father, a great clockmaker. The little boy became homeless and lived in a large clock by a train station in France. He had a burning desire to make this robot work that had the mechanisms of a clock within. These clockwork robots where able to perform a task that was so remarkable in many ways. He knew if he could make the robot work again it would reveal a message from his long lost father. Ultimately, the message revealed a very early movie in the history of filmmaking. It was George Melies, 'Le Voyage Dans La Lune.' The image is of a rocket ship hitting the man on the moon in the left eye. George Melies made many movies about dreams or being in the dream world. During the movie, Hugo discovers that the local vendor at the train station, who had been giving him a hard time, was in fact, George Melies, who had been hidden away from the public after the war. This is revealed when the picture of the moon and rocket is drawn by the robot and the healing of George Melies comes into play. In the movie, his many works are recovered and brought back to the conscious world again. The topic of dreamtime spoke to me. As a student at Emerson College, much later in my life, films like this or other Avante Garde filmmakers of the turn of the century paved the way to storytelling and non-ordinary realities well before my current life. Hugo discovers that the message from his father was to free the life existence of Melies and open our hearts once again to the dream world. When we are closed to the dream world we cease to communicate with the higher realms and other dimensional existences that are speaking to us and are there to help us on our journey of life, realization and higher states of consciousness.

I don't apologize for these segues in my story because this is how it all works. Sometimes a seemingly unrelated event suddenly becomes an integral piece of the puzzle to the deeper mysteries of what I have been trying to unveil throughout my life. In some respect, I can relate to the quest of Hugo who cannot stop until the answer is revealed. In my many spiritual insights and the closure to one question many other questions arise and then I have a burning desire to search for the answers and the clues of the mysteries that the universe wants to unveil. As Hugo persisted in saying, "I need to know what my father is telling me." I also need to know what my Heavenly Father is telling me what to do and what He wants me to share. The greater questions of, Why are we here? Who is God? Is there a God? What is our purpose? Why are there wars?...are a part of an endless list of powerful questions that have confounded the human race for many generations, In addition, as a seer and hearer, I have messages from others who may want to share their knowledge with the world. These messages will be revealed later in my story. Please keep in mind that the seer meets many visitors along the path and it is the job of the seer to describe, with accuracy, what this message is that may impact me or a greater portion of the population. The seer is merely the conduit and remains objective without judgment. The messenger is merely the seer. The wisdom always comes from above.

Chapter Three

A Spark From The Heavens

My Junior High years were somewhat uneventful except for the loss of my father. I was now embarking upon the entrance of my young adulthood. Now a high school student, I was able to make many of my own decisions. My mother had a much more relaxed approach to child rearing and after many discussions I was able to convince her that I was responsible for my actions, level headed and a fairly good student. Her only concern was that I was naive toward strangers and those who I should be more guarded with. Of course she was correct in her assessment of me. I was very mature in many ways and yet there was an innocence or childlike behavior that was a part of my personality. I blame it on the mist in the violets and grass from my childhood. It was a playful part of me that got into mischief. I could hide my slightly bad behavior under an innocent look of naivete. This allowed me to get into the type of mischief I wanted. Now I was able to begin my exploration of boys as they had caught up with me in height. Boys, boys, boys, oh yes, and more boys. I had finally hit puberty and it was time for me to leave off where I was in Junior High before the evil fairies of summer had cursed me with rapid growth of a fictional Alice-in-Wonderland's mundane life.

Weekends became filled with parties, local dances, and dates at the local restaurants and movie theaters. Large groups of classmates met at the brook, or the square or even the reservoir. Some had parties at their homes and some had the local hang outs in their basements. We had a full life of activities. There was always a place to go and an older boyfriend who had a car to take me there. Life was good! I can't complain about my high school years because I had fun. I feel sorry for those who can't say the same. It can be a real social and exciting time for teenagers, and I think it is unfortunate when people feel left out or bullied. I'm sure this happened in my school but I didn't see a whole lot of it. I will at least credit many of my classmates as being intelligent and comfortable enough with themselves that they didn't need to put other people down to feel better about themselves. I felt many were quality people who moved on to contribute something nice to society even if it was merely raising another generation of kind, understanding and tolerant people. No one really got hurt during those years, with the exception of a few unfortunate accidents.

Life was very good and I felt happy for the most part. We had our challenges with money since we were now a part of a single-parent home. I began babysitting for extra income and eventually started working at the local Ben Franklin's five and dime store. I loved working with the public because it gave me the opportunity to see a lot of people I knew or even meet a few new people along the way. I got many other jobs that were local and found it easy to keep in touch with those who wanted to reach me. I worked at pizza shops and a local homemade ice cream shop where I eventually became the manager. In school I began to excel in art and philosophy. I took a fashion design class and was creating my own clothing while I learned the basic skills of sewing. My mother was quick to encourage my interests in these areas as she had always expressed a desire to become a fashion designer. She was also an incredible artist and could draw with a clear exactness to the object on display. I, on the other hand, had a more sloppy form of expression with a mixed expression of likeness. Not quite her style as she would correct and remind me of the perspective and scale of the objects I was trying to match in my drawing. I suppose I could have gotten better at the skill of drawing but I knew I didn't have the patience to hone this skill as it should be. Instead, I would reflect upon the masters of color, shadow and light of the less structured brilliance of the French impressionists. I never felt I achieved any artistic level of accomplishment. However, I did receive a scholarship for art school from my two male art teachers who told me I should "exploit my talents." They seemed to be intrigued by my 'out-of-the-box' approach to my work. They would probably smile if they saw that I was drawing illustrations as an adult. I'm grateful for good teachers and am quick to show appreciation for any positive feedback since I never took myself seriously enough to achieve anything of substance or importance. We all have difficult teacher experiences and other adults who we encounter in our youth who at times display a level of cruelty or partiality that is detrimental to us and may have caused insecurities or hang ups. These are the memories that I have chosen to forget, forgive and send back to the universal karmic place where lessons needed to be learned. The people who I may have wronged in the past have now been karmically fulfilled.

My day to day high school experiences had their normal ups and downs of teenage frustrations, gossip, competitiveness, jealousy and headaches. I tried to make the best of it and felt that it was typical and similar to millions of others across the country. Everything would have been smooth sailing and I could have easily marked off my surreal childhood experiences as nothing more than fantasy...until it happened again.

We were on a school field trip when a handful of my classmates stood by a field and watched a white orb moving up and down a field of corn. I knew I saw it and to my surprise others saw it as well. I was finally relieved to know that I was not seeing things. The others were so upset that they kept denying they saw it and when we pointed out where the orb was they would shake their head in disbelief. Now that I knew this thing was visible to the outside world I suggested we get one of the teachers to see it. The rest of my classmates thought it wouldn't be a good idea in the event that the teacher couldn't see it and then force all of us to go to some type of counseling or psychological evaluation. I thought to myself, it's great to be surrounded by people who are intelligent enough to foresee some potential problem that could arise from this. All of us were content to keep it to ourselves and I never talked to anyone about it again.

I remember feeling very intrigued by the orbs. This was a time before we really heard about the crop circles. If there were any crop circles nearby, I never heard about them. I do know that the fast moving orb in and around the fields was identical to how the crop circle enthusiasts described the events. Yes, phenomenon occurred in Massachusetts, a long distance from the famous Stonehenge site of England.

Which brings me to another topic. I know they call this New England but much of the phenomenon of England was part of my early childhood experiences: King Arthur's Mists of Avalon; interpretation of mists in the violets and grassy lawn of my neighbors home; the pixies and fairies of the British Isles; extra-terrestrials and orbs of British crop circles; earth bound women from the witch trials....it was all too strange to me. The only exception may have been the Romans who seemed to have no specific connection to the Celtic origin or British Isles.

Why me? I don't have a connection to any of this. I will admit I had a bit of envy toward the Irish step dancers. Being of Italian descent, I couldn't participate in that fun dance and the pretty green dresses with the ringlet curls and bows. My ancestry was far removed to any of this type of magic and lore. No one taught me to believe in a leprechaun or fairy. I would look for an occasional four leaf clover but it was more generic in my attempt. The bottom line was that no one taught me anything about this so I had to come to the conclusion that I was highly connected to these other realms that had nothing to do with my heritage. Past life...hmmmm. That didn't fit into my Catholic upbringing either. What was this all about? Then another memory came back to me. It was someone in my childhood memory who talked to me about the karmic wheel. It feels like it was an adult. Oh, now I remember. A teacher at school told us about the Hindu belief of reincarnation during one of our classes. I keep thinking it may have been a substitute teacher. Remember, the Beatles really opened our culture up to Eastern religions and some of these philosophies had found their way into classrooms across the nation. This was a good thing to help expand our thoughts and the possibilities of other beliefs that can explain other types of realities and assist us on our path. Being exposed to other perspectives allows us to view the idea of sin or karma in a way that may have more meaning and value to our understanding.

So, getting back to the karmic wheel, I remember standing in my neighborhood and in a day vision observed this enormous wheel moving and spinning in time and the feeling of many people dying and then incarnating back into the wheel. It was a strange feeling of truth and so contrary to what I was being taught in catechism or Catholic school. I was troubled by it. I remember saying, " What if this is all true?" " What if everything is recorded in time and we need to do this all over again." I felt a sinking feeling in my gut and my mind began to race…I need to change something. I began to scan my own life searching in the dark places that hid all the darkest of intent, the unforgiveness, the cruelties, the human attributes of manipulation, jealousy and anger. I began to see incidences that revealed my guilt, my sin, my karma. I asked for forgiveness and the vision ended. I was told to stop doing what I was doing and to correct my behavior. It was all so surreal. It seemed to happen in a flash of time. I was standing around, children playing, and I was observing them play a game while viewing this third eye movie that played as a visual layer overlapping my space of human reality. No one said a word to me to interrupt this strange phenomenon. It seemed like it went on for 15 to 20 minutes but it was only seconds that the dream occurred. There was a strange time lapse or distortion of time that was unexplained. The mercy of the wise ones had given me a choice to correct my errors or ignore the information. I chose to exercise my free will of choice and correct my errors while asking for forgiveness of bad decisions from the past. It all disappeared as quickly as it arrived. Similar to a dream, it was so clear in the beginning when one awakes and the memory slips rapidly from the conscious mind. Why is it that some memories disappear so quickly and others are remembered in detail? I am also surprised that I had not remembered that moment for many years and here we are, I'm telling you about my story and it is as fresh in my memory as if it happened just moments ago.

Years before this illumination I recalled a time when my oldest brother brought us to see see a Yogi who had visited the states. He blessed me and introduced me to my own personal mantra. I felt good about the session and my oldest brother claimed he felt a lot of peace while experiencing transcendental meditation. I may have been 7 or 8 years old at the time. I don't doubt that this was an early induction that was a part of my path in my formative years to enable me to do what I do today. The Eastern religions have helped me in so many ways. Even today, I conduct a meditation class to help others find this peace of mind that everyone should experience as part of a spiritual transformational process.

Which leads me to another unexplained incident... I can't describe what this was other than a feeling like nothing else on Earth. I had been talking to friends or my older sister who had been involved in a Protestant or Pentecostal church. My philosophical and religious curiosity brought me to many places. I recall sitting in a philosophy class discussing the third and fourth dimensions and multiple planes of existence. It helped to broaden my perspective and examine the spiritual realities from different angles or points of reference. The thought of visiting a new church was curious. The thought of being born again was interesting. I didn't even attend a church when the universe presented me with an idea and a question. Do I love God? At the time I wasn't sure if there was a God. The educational system had ruled much of this out of the picture to lay a groundwork for evolution. When looking back on these teachings I can't help but think that there was so much history and archeological information that I think we were robbed of the opportunity to make our own decisions as many factual pieces were not included in the final evaluation. That's not education, that is eliminating many historical and scientific theories to support only one biased theory that places us in a basic food chain within the animal kingdom. We'll get into this much later. However, I knew that there was something more out there that was not easy to explain. The rotation of the planets and the orbits of the galaxy alone seemed to rule out the disorderly order of the big bang theory. It wasn't until the brilliant mind of the quantum physicists did we begin to see the real picture. I don't want to live in the Dark Ages anymore or listen to the teachers who still want us to believe the Earth is flat. Let's let go of a missing link theory of hopeful explanations when the Ancient Sumerians have already explained where we come from, thousands of years ago.

Getting back to the moment I asked if there was a God. I fell into a deep sleep with the intention to open my heart to God if there is one to reach out to. I saw a book, a journal that I had written in just moments before this sleep fell over me. I had written, "I love God." I was just 15 years old and had no other intent other than my quest for the truth. The writing took place again in my dream and I was transfixed between two worlds as a rush of energy so profound came over me and I was immobilized. Gasping for breath, I couldn't move, and without notice another wave of emotion filled my soul as if someone had brought me back to life as if I had been previously dead. Tears streamed down my face, and I saw myself laying on my bed. There were no words to explain what just happened. It didn't matter because I couldn't speak anyhow. It was early evening and I stepped outside of my bedroom, stunned and still tears flowing from my eyes I didn't know what was happening. My mother heard me step from the bedroom and her eyes opened up wide.

Mother: What just happened to you?

Arael: I don't know, I just wrote on my journal, "I love God."

Mother: You are glowing! You look like an angel!

I was confused and it all felt awkward. I didn't want my mother to think I was something other than her child. I dismissed her comments and said,

Arael: "I don't know what just happened. I thought it was all a dream. I felt this wave of energy and then I couldn't move. I felt a bit frightened because it was so powerful and I don't have any idea why there are tears in my eyes."

My mother began to recognize that I was feeling uncomfortable and she suggested that I get some rest.

Nothing significant happened to me after that except for the communication in prayer had now opened up. I could hear the voice speaking to me and guiding me in my life. I had received an unexplained spark from the Heavens and I would never be the same again.

Chapter four

The Walk of Faith

Everything seemed to come together while I was in high school. I went to three proms and enjoyed a fun social life. My grades were above average and I had quite a few friends and many good memories. I had a tumultuous relationship with my son's father who was my high school boyfriend and yet, made the best of it all. For the most part, I didn't have much to complain about except for the fact that I would miss everyone from school. It was now time for all of us to take the next step into adulthood and apply for college. The autumn leaves of my senior year seemed richer and more bold than ever before. I felt a strong sense of accomplishment and the vibrant feeling of education was all around me. After all, Boston had so many colleges to pick from. What should I do with my life? There, in front of the school I would rest under the weeping willow tree overlooking the pond. This was my favorite place to rest. This was the place of my first kiss with my son's father. When I look at my son I can see his father's face at times and the kindness he had for me then. It is a good feeling and that is mixed with memories that will last forever. I can still feel the weight of the books and the challenges of learning. I must be honest and say that I can't recall a single math class and barely recall science. Yet, I can see myself gazing out the window during social studies, English and biology. I was still a dreamer watching the other students walk by outside the door sometimes waving or a boy flirting or looking in while saying something funny to interrupt the class. There were two social studies teachers who wouldn't stop harassing one another. It became a big game and an intentional form of entertainment for all of us. We sat there watching and waiting for the next sarcastic witty remark that caused the other teacher to rise up and come back with a comment to match his wit.

I remember the day that I decided I needed to be responsible and begin to think about college. My mother never pushed me in this direction. Yet, I knew that this was something I just had to do. Everyone in school seemed to be preparing for that next phase in their lives. Since I never really disliked academics, and the school environment was fun to me, I was enthusiastic about heading to college and began the application process.

Arael: I don't know what I want to do with my career? I like art but I can't be a starving artist.

Mother: You should be a fashion designer. Talk to your guidance counselor to see what school best fits your interests.

Arael: I'm not sure that I'm very good at sewing as you are. I like to design but I don't really like to sew like you do.

Mother: You need to find something to do. I'll bring you by the campus so you can see the school. I always wanted to be a designer and I think you will be good at it because you have some of my talents.

I knew she was proud of me. I would be the second child to go to college in our family. My oldest brother attended college and my other brother attended a prep school. All of this was a beautiful dream and I felt my future was very promising. It was all too perfect when I noticed there was something wrong. I was too young to have picked up the signs earlier. People began visiting my home more than usual and my mother seemed more withdrawn and tired. My mother had cancer...

I started to get worried. Where would I go? What should I do? Each day I came home she had more problems. By the spring of my senior year I knew I wasn't going to college. It was a point when I just about ready to leave the nest and explore life as a young adult. Instead, I stayed home and worked while I cared for my mother. Relatives and friends came over to transport her to the hospital for chemotherapy. It began with breast cancer and then spread to every part of the body, the brain, the blood, the lymph nodes, etc. It was very painful for her and I was grateful that I could care for her in the end. I remember her calling me in the middle of the night asking for a drink of water or help to the bathroom. I remember her wanting to talk or just watch television together. I remember her life force energy slip away as she became weaker and depleted by the cancer she couldn't fight off any longer. I never thought I sacrificed anything. I wouldn't have done it any other way. The day after she died, I woke up to her voice calling me. I heard her voice and knew she was still there. I walked by her bedroom slowly telling her I loved her and in time her voice disappeared as she left the earth plane and went into the light.

I know I grieved for my mother for almost 10 years after her death. I didn't have a desire to go back to school or any other aspirations of a career. Instead my eyes were set on spiritual things. I attended church and tried to sort out this trauma that I couldn't easily shake. After all, my mother understood me unlike anyone else around me. We were both very contemplative, thoughtful daydreamers. When she died, I had a sense of being lost. Maybe the connection we had while I was still in her womb was much stronger than I realized. I considered the regression and how I didn't feel like I had a separate identity as the other children ran around. I never felt that I had to be first or in the forefront amongst my siblings. There was a quiet sense of knowing that I was going to get cared for and I didn't have any anxiety about it. We had a telepathic sort of knowing that is hard to describe. Just as she put herself on the back burner, so did I. Now, being removed from the Earth plane I felt aimless in my efforts. Somehow and some way I needed to find out who I was separate from her. The local church persuaded me to go to Bible school and study theology. I knew I was ready for this journey and opened my heart up to it completely.

At the time, I cared for an elderly woman who's husband was a prominent military man in the Army. She claimed to have danced with Henry Ford at a Dearborn Michigan Country Club amongst other interesting things during her travels. I told her that I needed to attend Bible college and would be leaving her. Ironically I purchased a Ford Escort and was on my way to Bible College near Tulsa Oklahoma. It was half way across the country and then experienced a wonderful feeling of freedom. Back home, my elderly woman friend discovered she had cancer and she died months later.

I sat and thought about that for a long time. How many people in my life contracted cancer? Three of my grandparents, one died of old age, both my parents, an uncle and other relatives and now the older woman I cared for. This was very sad and disturbing at the same time. What was cancer...? It was something that bothered me for many years. As I grew older I helped people who had cancer in any way that I could and noticed that fewer people around me died pre-maturely later on in life.

When I stepped into Tulsa, I stepped into another country. They were so different from New Englanders that I couldn't find a common thread. The only thing that I remembered was the people. The southern drawl, the neat and perfectly groomed big hair. The cowboy hats and the bright colorful clothing. The healthy looking complexions and the friendly smiles. The most outstanding was a woman named Darla and her husband Jeff. Darla was just married and she was probably one of the kindest person I had ever met. When I arrived in town I stopped at a local restaurant and there she was, like pure sunshine, her face was honest and sincere. As soon as we met it was as if I had always known her. She was wonderful!

Darla: Hi there, would you like to get something to eat? Have you ever been here before?

Arael: No, I just drove out here from Massachusetts and I would like to get something to eat.

Darla: Wow, you're a long way from home. How long will you be staying here.

Arael: I'm here to attend the Bible School in town.

Darla: Isn't that a coincidence, that's where my husband and I are attending. Where are you going to stay while you live here?

Arael: I don't know I haven't figured that out yet.

Darla: What about work? Do you have a job yet?

Arael: No, I just got here today and my friend and I are staying at a local hotel for a week. Then she will be returning home by plane. After that, I will need to find some place to stay.

Darla: You could stay with us until you find something. We have an extra bedroom. They are looking for waitresses here at the restaurant. Do you want to apply for a job?

Immediately I was amazed by her generosity, helpfulness and kindness. She has to be an angel. No one is this nice! At least not without an agenda. So I talked to her a little more and looked into her eyes and saw that she was a real angel, blameless, honest and pure. I knew they sent me to her as I was obedient to take the path of spiritual learning. The job worked out fine and I lived with Darla and Jeff for six months. After that she helped me find a home to live in for another six months while they tried to sell the house. It was a real blessing. I didn't make much more than minimum wage and yet, I was making it. I was feeling optimistic about my life. I was feeling cared for and guided.

Another kind angel who walked into my life was an African American woman who referred to herself as Big Mary. I would call her Big Mama instead. She was the kindest soul and was always asking me if I needed help with anything. We had a love for one another as if we were family and enjoyed talking for hours. Aside from my Aunt, who I adore and love very much, Mary was probably Heaven's way of reminding me that Angels exist on Earth. I lost track of Big Mary because I had to move and keep going forward. However, I will never forget her kindness and learned how to have compassion with strangers.

I remember the landscape of Oklahoma. It was flat and had so much more open space. That was very different from anything else that I had ever experienced. Even the energy seemed strange as I could feel the pulse of the earth in various locations. There was a sense of freedom unlike the more bound and restricted feeling I had in New England. The freedom here undoubtedly matched the energy of the Plains Indians whose energy impacted the landscape with a sense of revelry, freedom, and uninhibited reckless abandon. Nothing could stand in the way of this energy as it proclaimed the power of an untamed Eagle in flight searching for it's prey and taking whatever it wanted. I experienced the glory of humanity and animal life cohabiting together in pure simplicity and synergy. There was a feeling of Oneness...a balance that seemed much more natural than the tight laws of Boston's early tea party taxes and the spiritual oppression that never quite left the area even after the war. If I could bottle this energy up and bring it back to set the captives free I would in an instant. I always thought it was amusing when Texans would boast about being bigger, better and claim to have prettier women. Well, I suppose that could be true and when I saw a football team walk through the restaurant I asked what college they were from. To my surprise they were from a local high school. I said, "Are you kidding, there isn't a player shorter than 6 feet tall. That's when I realized that they really weren't kidding.

Apart from being cared for, I really wasn't sure why I moved to Oklahoma. I know I was there to learn and become a spiritual teacher. I studied theology, church history and the Bible from front to back. There were ways to interpret the scriptures and I learned various methods, theories and what the school wanted me to understand. They could think well outside the box as I did. Sometimes they helped me come to my own conclusions and other times they felt very strongly regarding specific doctrines and beliefs. The school was helpful but I didn't have the spiritual connection I thought I would, as it had not been nearly as profound as what I had experienced in the past. Nothing really notable happened there except for the tornados that seemed to be an ongoing reality in this part of the country and an introduction to my husband who seemed highly charismatic. There was a specific time when tornados were dropping down around the area and the founder of the school proclaimed that he was a man of faith and God would always protect their school. The outcome was disastrous for many and a tornado dropped down on the very road where the school was and demolished all the buildings across the street. The school, on the other hand, was unscathed. Not even a piece of lumber, flower or shrub was affected. That was noteworthy and interesting to witness. Does that mean or prove that God had love for the school and had no regard for the people across the street? This was something to ponder and I will leave it there. I understand that in the eyes of the universe we all have intrinsic value.

Just the thought of the tornadoes was amazing to me. The sound they made, the unusual wall clouds of a bright turquoise color in a thick blanket overlooking a town or city. It was powerful force to be reckoned with. It was a strange natural wind tunnel that could drop down in small clusters of funnel clouds, destroy a small space or area, and rise up at any given moment without touching anything else around it.

My husband was ten years my senior, charismatic and had a unique talent for being able to entertain any crowd of people. I would always see him at school with a circle of people around him as he would share or talk about his insights of the Bible. He was respected for his knowledge and could meet people without trying.

Before I met him, he was an evangelist who served many years in the military as a military police officer overseas. At a turning point in his life he got involved in the church as an evangelist. His future as a minister was very promising. He had all the attributes of a polished Pentecostal Evangelist. He could draw in the attention of a crowd and kept them dangling on his every word. His heart seemed pure and the desire to help others evolved into many long hours of conversations to those around us in need.

We enjoyed each others company and had a similar sense of humor and love for God. Even though I was aware that I didn't have a deep love for him, we got married anyhow. The age difference between us created an environment of a mild power struggle as he would assert himself by trying to parent me with an added list of rules and controls that I wasn't accustomed to. Being a free spirit, I felt very unhappy and restricted. This became more of a problem later in time because I was still grieving the loss of my mother and just tolerated a lot.

We settled into his home town in Nebraska. Seven years went by quickly and my desire to spread my wings again stirred me to rebellion. Before the completion of seven years, I had another spiritual awakening...

The quietness of a sleepy Nebraska town was so slow paced that I could hear myself think. Landscapes of cornfields stirred my imagination and I remember walking through the fields of corn with a surge of energy like none other. The expansive fields that rolled and curved like aisles of green and yellow linear paths, created an emotion of unfamiliar euphoria in me. I could never quite explain this feeling. Growing up near Boston, I had never viewed a landscape so breathtaking, as it was completely untouched and in unity with nature...I had to take it all in. I scanned the entire field 360 degrees around. It all went on for miles while being crisscrossed by dirt roads and outdated worn down pickup trucks. It was the energy there that spoke to me. It was the Earth itself that was breathing into my soul. I would gasp and breath in the very life of the Earth and began to heal the depths of my heart and spirit. I watched my very being fill like water being poured into a glass and almost overflowing.

With time on my hand, as time almost seemed to stand still there. We were frozen to the rest of the world, without constant interactions of others and many hours to kill time, I began to read. Being compelled by curiosity, my mind never stood still and I was on a quest for knowledge. I read old religious texts like the Anti-Nicene Fathers and learned about early church martyrs and various Protestant movements. I found myself reading many books from the 1600s written by early Puritans. Years later, I discovered that I had been a Puritan minister who turned on his own clergy to defend the British Crown. If I was not that minister, then I know that I was there somehow in that lifetime. The Puritan writings were not an easy read and most people shied away from the length of descriptions that were interspersed with archaic words and terminology. I could read it and understand it easily. I felt all the writers were my friends. Imagine, a 20 something year old woman reading the writings of Puritans? None of this made sense. My fervor for Shakespeare and Chaucer were also strange and my love for Mozart, Beethoven, Bach, Handel and more...I was not looking to enhance my culture but saw my tastes change dramatically. I was old when I was young and I became young when I was much older.

The Native people made a strong impression on me. It started in Oklahoma when I saw them in full regalia and proudly walking in various places throughout towns and cities. I remember reading about the great Cherokee Chief Sequoyah who created the Cherokee Alphabet and the how this language was preserved. In Nebraska I attended Pow Wows of the Omaha Tribe. There was one instant where I was seated on a bleacher, observing the ceremony, when I noticed a native elder staring at me in the seat opposite the bleachers. There weren't many people on the bleachers and I was aware that he was looking specifically at me. It was as if he was in a trance. His eyes were transfixed upon my eyes and I felt this strange sense of hypnosis or a magnetic locking-in-effect. I couldn't shift my eyes and move away. I was being downloaded by something or someone that this elder was channeling. Then he broke the stare and walked away. It felt like it went on forever but it may have been 7 or 8 minutes long. It's really hard to tell in a situation like this unless you are observing the time before and after. No one said a word. My husband, who never missed anything, didn't notice and I was relieved because I knew that this was something unexplainable and not how he could have interpreted it. Soon after that Pow Wow the visions began or as some would say, my third eye had opened.

The part that was interesting was that I did not open up and have visions of native people or warriors of the Plains. Instead my window opened up to Tibet. I felt the oppression of a group of Chinese men who wanted to harm me. I didn't understand it. It was as if there was an old conflict that I didn't remember and I could hear their verbal threats distinctly along with the sounds of a water torture that went on for days. I would go to lay down at night or day and I would hear their taunting voices and the sound of dripping water by my head at every waking moment. I could see them at times and then it would return back to the sound. Eventually, through prayer, the tormenters went away.

I believe that souls do not die and they can be Earthbound for many lifetimes returning to find people they had problems with in the past. When I opened up into the spirit realm I could finally hear their voices and harassments that accompanied it. This, undoubtedly had been a part of my personal torment and nightmare for years, but I was finally open enough for it to be revealed.

After I lifted this from me I began to see angels and had other surreal dreams of another being. I call him a being because I don't believe he was human. He threatened me in a lucid dream that was so real and intimidating to such a degree that I could hardly move when I awakened. I believe he may have been from a galactic council and he challenged me as if I was interfering with a greater plan that he had in mind. I can only identify with this being because he showed up much later and revealed that he was one of the leaders of a galactic council and that they were asserting themselves as a powerful force on the Earth. Here again, I was finally able to see them and for that reason there was an interaction and reminder of who should be in power. This was done through a process of intimidation. I didn't challenge them. I would listen to what they had to say and then try to read between the lines. Some would say that this is absurd. As powerful as this collective consciousness was or claimed to be, none of it mattered because they could never harm me or anyone else in this dimension again. I imagine they had their reign but would soon discover that humans were now becoming more awakened and not as vulnerable to their requests of dominance. The Origin Beings and the God Source still reign in power. All else must find their place in the strata of spiritual hierarchy of the many dimensional realms of order.

Here again, I had opened the door, or should I say, the native elder helped me open it. This went on for months. I was sent through a swirling wind of non-ordinary reality as we know it. None of it was pleasant and it was like spiritual awakening to a nightmare. I thought, I don't want to see or hear anymore. I want to be free from it. I couldn't shake the grips of this experience as I called out to the angels for help.

My husband and I decided to take a trip to South Dakota to visit the Badlands. I remember seeing this place and feeling spiritually uplifted. I loved the amazing hills of sandy rock layers mixed in green, golds and burnished reds that twisted upward like ribbon candy. The sun rising upon the sandy, rocky, and mineral laden landscape created glittering effects of diamonds strewn throughout the walls of the dipping craters. I knew this place. I remembered the freedom as I ran to a jetting edge that allowed me to look further into this crater. I was transformed and felt as if I had taken flight. I sat there and could hear my husband's voice fading deeper into nothingness. Fearless in my thoughts, I sat near the edge. He thought, in moments of anxiety as he watched me whimsically float to the edge that I might have been considering thoughts of suicide. In truth, that was the farthest thing from my mind. I held on to this experience while inhaling the air and surrounding my visual frame of only me and the Earth. It was as if heaven had met me at the pearly gates. I know most people would not have this same experience as I did. It could be that by the grace of God I found myself and my connection to God that had been lost so many lifetimes before. It was a renewed trust and hope of a brighter future. During the time there I began to receive insight about my life now and for the first time I had a clear channel to my highest good. The last message I received was that it was time for me to return to Boston and get a divorce. They had other plans for me and I should not be in a situation where I am prevented from doing what it was being asked to do. I recognized that I had fallen away from my life purpose and it was time for me to get back on track.

The next memory was on my plane ride home. It was sobering and I had no idea what was up ahead of me. I let go of my solitude in the Plains and cornfields of Nebraska and returned to the high energy of Massachusetts again. Little did I know I had so much karma and unfinished business ahead of me. My only desire was to escape this non-ordinary reality and for a while I actually did.

Chapter Five

Past life During the Civil War

Now that I had returned to Boston I had a different type of whirlwind overtake me. It was a huge shift from being in the slow paced environment of the Midwest and then to walk into a much more high paced busy lifestyle of Boston. I returned home to visit and to file for a divorce. The epiphany of realizing that I should leave my husband during my visit to the Badlands had changed me forever. I would never forfeit my freedom and live under anyone else's rule for the remainder of my life. Being a free spirit I could now begin to explore life and the challenges of both the good and the bad that life had to offer.

It was such a hard transition and the cost of living seemed almost double from what I had been accustomed to. The first thing I did was Immerse myself into work. Not having a degree in higher education I worked in the restaurant industry. I was starting my life all over. I didn't have any children at the time and I began to develop new friendships. My family became my cornerstone as I began my life from scratch. With new found freedom and a return to my old stomping grounds, I began to search for familiar faces from my past. I caught up with old classmates who were married and had children. There I was, single, divorced and no children. A part of me wanted what they had and a part of me didn't. I think I was just spreading my wings and the thought of slowing down now seemed less appealing. Out of curiosity, I looked up my childhood sweetheart who had not gotten married or had any children. We decided to start dating again but that wasn't working out. The same disagreements we had as teenagers were still unresolved. Nevertheless, we had a child together and tried to make it work. With the challenges of life and a young baby in hand, I found that we were too engaged in arguments and other issues that were not good for a healthy environment of rearing a child. Both of us were on the fence and at odds with unending contrasting opinions. My astrologer friends reminded me that a Cancer and Capricorn relationship typically doesn't work. We are on the completely opposite ends of the Zodiac and somewhere in the middle was our Aquarian child.

I'm a bit of a stargazer, not necessarily one to analyze the constellations or to read my future. I look to the stars and see my home. This is the other place that captures my heart as strongly as the Earth. It comforts me like a blanket of love and I awaken to the sounds of birds singing amongst the trees. I have always been one foot in this world and one foot out. It has never been intentional for me to be that way but rather the defining part of who I am. I strongly believe that we will all be in this place and this is an indication of being connected in the right way to the God source. It is available to everyone and I will say that there is such a peace in this existence that I could never express in words.

When the stars opened up to me I began to see into the Akashic records. This is the place where I found the recorded history of my soul's incarnation on Earth as well as other dimensional realms. I believe all of us have some form of communication from this realm to remind our soul that we have been here before and that we are being reminded that the present time is our exploration of life from a different perspective that we had not previously experienced. It is a gift to incarnate and live the human experience with all the many blessings and trials that go along with it. Everyone has moments of dreams or deja vu or other odd spiritual experiences that remind us that we have been here before. Most of the time we ignore these dreams because they are merely to serve as a reminder that our life decisions matter and we have a unique purpose and value to contribute to the world around us, even if it is just being who we are. The higher realms encourage us to live in the here and now and to not get bogged down with the past, unless this is the lifetime where we need to deal with clearing our karma. If we cry out from our soul that we need answers as to why we are here, or why we had so many difficult challenges in our life, then the Universe will direct us to people and places that will help us understand what we need to learn to release the challenges we now face. Everyone is met at the door of sincere soul-searching requests.

I had many dreams and visitations in my life. Non-ordinary reality was something I had been experiencing all along. Yet, the next experience I had startled me to such a degree that it shook my very soul. I felt the power of the universe that reminded me of my fragile human existence that could be dusted away like a speck of sand. This vision brought me to my knees and I collapsed within myself knowing that nothing is greater than the powers above.

I was walking down the street and aware of my surroundings, yet troubled by the many challenges I had faced during my life time. My mind was fixed on finding solutions or understanding why this was all happening. Suddenly a window opened within my third eye a placement of movie screen was revealed. It was holographic as if I could see this dimension of space and simultaneously observe my natural surroundings of cars, people, stores and the typical scenery of a small New England town.

The movie began to play as I was transported into the timeline of the Civil War, somewhere down south. I had strong feelings that this all took place in Georgia soon after the Civil War had ended. I could see myself, a natural golden blonde haired woman with my hair pulled up and strands of curls fell gently down the back and on the sides near my cheek. I was wearing a beautiful long dress that was very worn out. It appeared to be pink but I knew it was a beautiful red dress at one time. I knew I was a daughter of a wealthy plantation owner who had many slaves and servants. The war had been so devastating. We had lost everything as our home was burned to the ground by riotous Yankees who had made a strong presence after the war. Those Yankee Soldiers completed their work by burning down or even pillaging the wealth of former slave owners. I imagine that slaves were not treated fairly. However, as a young woman in the house, many of the house servants or slaves were my friends.

Our devastating loss caused my father and me to live on a homestead near a small body of water or lake. The land owner of that property somehow retained his power and was brutal to all who fell under his control. He was a handsome man with a charming personality and strong political connections. He had wavy brown hair with streaks of grey running through it, a dignified look on his face, an aquiline nose, a strong chin and cheekbones and a prominent brow. His clothing was conservative at the time and he wore gray jackets of tidy tailored suits and ascot ties with pedigree details. He would entertain families who had endured the war and kept their strongholds in place. It didn't matter to him how other families were destroyed. He took this as a sign of weakness and saw it as an opportunity to gain more wealth and land. My family's land was confiscated by him and we were fully subservient to his whims. Years earlier, I had rejected him as a gentleman caller and he had an anger from rejection that couldn't be quenched. I was frequently mistreated by this man, both emotionally and sexually until his anger reached a height from my endless rejection of his disillusioned affection. The scene was murderous and full of a monstrous hatred that I could never forget. He lashed out with a vengeance to destroy the face of rejection he could never accept. A brutal murder took place and I observed my body floating on the water as he rode away in blood guilt fear.

The tears were streaming down my eyes as I witnessed what had happened to me. The pain of it all was too harsh to view. What was going on! I shouted in my mind as the screen shut down like a movie theatre closes down the show. The window was now closed and the hologram was now gone. Desperate in my thoughts, I looked to see if anyone had observed me during this horrendous meltdown. I glanced across the street and looked ahead and behind me. No one seemed to notice or care. It was as if I was oblivious to the world and only the universe and I knew what had just happened.

The questions began to reel in my head. What is happening to me? Why am I seeing these things. The answers began to come in as I looked at my life much differently now. I felt that everything I did was being recorded, and that my decisions would determine my future outcome. I was not to just float through space but rather find out what is the best path for me.

Still, I was not satisfied regarding the vision. How can I see something like this and what was this all about. Later I discovered that I could peer into this realm to help others find their answers as well. At this time I was not prepared to help anyone because I needed time to understand my own reality first. The entrance into this profound experience made me want to hide again from the spiritual experiences that continued to visit my life in so many unexpected ways. My wish to have a simple life was granted to me and the higher Beings allowed a few more years before they would knock on my door again.

What happened the next few years was an array of human challenges with my sons father that manifested in many life lessons of conflicting parental views, disagreements and more. My son was a young child who still remembered the ways of the Heavens and reminded us that he loved the both of us equally. Children have an interesting way of shedding light on very dismal topics. They are our gift and feed our souls with joy that is beyond imagination. A similar feeling can be expressed or appreciated through the animal kingdom, who have the same God type of innocence and unconditional love that is impossible to describe. These are our gifts on the planet and both children and animals should be highly protected and guarded by us to insure that this innocence continues to hold the divine space on the Earth.

My journey continued to help me understand the human experience and learn from the many different types of people who come from all walks of life, races, belief systems and traditions. It was pleasant at times and quite difficult as well. I learned mostly about myself and tried to adjust many behaviors that needed to change. I grew and when I had another lesson to be learned, I struggled until I came to terms with it or learned to forgive. When I walked in the reality of forgiveness, everything began to come together for me. This was the freedom I had been searching for. This was the release of my many karmic ties that were falling away from me and drawing me up into the skies. This part of my journey took many years, and I had many past life dreams and hints of spiritual awakening along the way.

Chapter Six

Meditation Minded

The life in the suburbs of a New England town was filled with activities. Children and their sports, school and friends dominated a good portion of my daylight hours. I drove from place to place and interacted with parents, committees, teams and more. The concerns of homework, training, dinner time, travel, and communication was the key points of reality. I worked and juggled every waking moment into a frenzy of non-stop business. I don't believe I heard myself think for nearly a decade. Of course, there were moments of spirituality that crept in through unexpected moments of reflection. None of which were truly coherent in the same way that I had processed things in the past. The quietness of my earlier part of my life had me so connected to other realms that I seemed to have an idea of where I stood with God.

The endless cycle of this reality put me in a spiritual daze to the point that I no longer recognized who I was. There was a vacancy and disparaging thoughts of difficult situations kept rising up before me. The competitive environment cast me out into a swirling abyss of anger as I viewed behaviors that were so unsavory that I began to resent the life that I was living and the unfortunate experiences that my son would have to deal with.

I wanted out of this rat race and didn't remember where to go to find refuge. I plummeted deep within an endless pit of nothingness with a feeling of void and emptiness around me. My emotions of negativity were beginning to affect my son and he also began to lose his zeal for life. At this fortress, I was being forced to charge the drawbridge or surrender. But who am I to surrender to? Suddenly I realized how far I had strayed from my path and remembered the urgency to get back to my spiritual sense of knowing.

I ventured over to a metaphysical store to find something to sooth my mind when I realized there was a meditation class beginning within a few minutes. Out of desperation, I chose to join the group and this was the key to reconnecting to my spiritual communication.

The classes introduced me to a more formal way to clear my heart, my chakras and my third eye, that had closed in darkness when I made the integration back into a material world. I had to be reminded what I already knew and that I should be prepared for other experiences that were too difficult to explain.

I spent hours of meditation to help me find inner peace. The practice of mediumship was also a part of the class and I began to incorporate that part to help validate my intuition and recognize if the information had a level of accuracy. To my surprise, much of this came easy to me as if it were my second nature. The hunger and thirst for more only added more peace and insight. Being surrounded by like-minded people, became an added bonus. I literally floated along this path for a while, maybe 6 months or so, in a whimsical bliss of tantalizing realities.

Then, the visions became more prominent and so were the souls from other dimensions. I was calling forth the very things I had run away from many years earlier. I was now better prepared and less frightened by strange happenings occurring around me. The ancient teachings of Mysticism, Hinduism, Buddhism, and other Eastern religions and metaphysical thought helped me better understand my earlier experiences. It was also wonderful to speak with people who had experienced other dimensional realities as I had. My life began to light up like a field full of fire flies. I dove into this reality with open arms and a pure heart, finally recognizing that I could help others with my gift of sight.

The daydreams had also opened up to night dreams as I had an unexplained vision of a mighty angel hovering over me during my waking hours while in my bed. The magnificence and power of him was overwhelming. No one could explain what I was seeing and I came to terms with it all. It is what it is...

I stopped worrying about how these things were happening and also why it was happening. Instead, I started to just flow with it and the visions came in stronger and more prominent. I began to record and document what I was experiencing. Other strange things happened such as my writing ability had changed and I began writing in a style that I had never learned or practiced. The poetry that flowed from my memory of the violets in the grass, had emerged as delightful stories for children, that I believed came from the elemental realm of the Fae. At times I would hear their voices and giggle as they told me what they wanted me to say. They love children in such a way that the world couldn't believe or imagine. They know how to make them happy and nurture their sense of joyfulness and laughter in a very imperfect world.

Other voices began to chime in as friends from the other side dictated to me stories of another kind that were more suited for adults. I wrote them all down and published a few to share with others. They all had a deeper meaning or lesson to be learned from within our human experience. These were voices of our guardians of light, the keepers of the books, the winged creatures of the heavens,the gossamer wing types from the subterranean earth, the mischievous leprechauns and elves from our childhood, were all reaching out to be heard once again and to heal our hungry souls. These spirits can return us to our childhood happiness where we once found the Earth and it's surrounding to be so wonderfully innocent, mystical and magical.

I became intrenched in the tedious task of writing everything down and organizing all the stories in groups. This took up many hours and years of compiling, but I never begrudged the work that they asked me to do. I never knew if there would be any return on this. I did it out of love for the beings who were sent to help us, to shed light on the mysteries of life and entertain us with their silliness. I wasn't a martyr. I would describe myself more as a silly daydreamer. Accuse me, as they may, I will be determined to remain this way! I was probably the happiest I had ever been and would not have forfeited this time in my life for anything else the world could have offered.

In the middle of all of these experiences came a group of guides I called The Riddlers. These were my guides who wanted to show me synchronicity in life to reveal connections that I had never considered. I was never the type to explore much of anything or investigate in any depth until this began happening to me. The thought of tediously making connections seemed like more work than I wanted to delve into. I liked when things were very straightforward and required little research. Never in a million years had I expected to get into something of this nature. Similar to the rest of my insights, I began to document my findings and would write down what was presented to me. At times they would direct me to the internet where there is a tremendous wealth of information. I would hear a lead, a name, or other detail, and then go and search in a way that they wanted me to. Within a few hours or over a short period of time, I could find the connections they wanted me to see and solve or discover something that I had never known or read about. This became more interesting after I began to read the Akashic records and more information would flow to me while I was in the records and many times it would continue well after until the task was completed. After a while, I didn't have to search the Akashic records, it would just come to me like a flood of information. In a very strange way, I felt that I was healing from these investigative insights. Somehow I was feeling a sense of closure and thought it was a very strange experience. Many of the incidences I unearthed did not necessarily apply to me directly but rather it felt like I was opening the door to insight regarding unsolved universal mysteries that needed to come forth. I began to see the value in this and started to share with others. They too had interesting, "ah ha " moments and seemed to experience what I was experiencing. My guess was that I had been directed to a way to help in the process of universal Akashic findings that could help release or allow healing in a time of great pain, sorrow, or confusion. I wasn't sure but I knew that it never had a negative affect but rather something always occurred that was positive. Even if people didn't believe what I had seen, and I was willing to accept that, I still sensed that something would change around them since they had to also search within to find the topic we addressed. When they searched within, they made a connection to the divine within themselves. I was pleased to be a part of this process.

I began doing private readings to practice with friends and then many began to call me for readings. My work evolved into workshops and weekly classes. I published my first book, ***Macabre****, short stories and poems from the other side* and *Green Stories for Green Children.* I wasn't sure whether or not I was successful but I did feel happy inside to be able to share all of these experiences.

My journey has taken me to so many places and I was happy to return to being who I was and to enjoy the journey all the way. This voyage to the other side and back has been a very interesting experience and so I take many voyages into the other realms to see what they are saying to us in the present time.

Chapter Seven

The Riddlers

The place of non-ordinary reality brought me to what I refer to as The Riddler's. They are the ones who give me information piece by piece and ask me to solve the puzzle. It can be a combination of synchronicity, imagery, symbology, and other forms of hidden meaning. They will visit me in my meditation and give me hints, sometimes one at a time. This is not too much dissimilar to the unraveling of secret societies that uses layers of meaning attached to symbols that define a specific belief or view and speaks without talking. Telling tales of the past and hidden links to our future can be quite intriguing.

I recall being in a mediumship class when I looked at a man across from me and saw him in the past. He was wearing a patriot outfit but I knew all along that he was in fact a pirate. He stood there waiting by a landscape of evergreen trees near the ocean while his pirate crew started unloading some of the treasures from his ship. It felt like it was in New Hampshire or northern New England. The man I was observing, being an intuitive as well, insisted that this took place somewhere in South America. I didn't agree because the landscape was accurately New England. However, we were both in agreement that the coins that he was burying into the ground were Spanish Doubloons. I said to the man in my class, "You were a pirate dressed as a patriot and I see you after you had stolen some gold from the King of Spain during that time." Fascinated by it, he looked deeply and gathered the information he needed or didn't need. My strongest feeling was that he had encountered something far greater than the daring life of a rebel pirate. Months later I heard a story begin to churn and a release of words unfolded into a story that came in crystal clear from my inner ears. Prescott's waiting...

Arael: Prescott's Waiting? Who said that?

Voice: Prescott's waiting!

Arael: Prescott's Waiting for what?

Voice: Prescott's waiting for help. There are soul pieces to retrieve for the sailors of the sea. You will know who they will be when you unleash the curse from Poseidon's prison by the sea.

Arael: What should I do? Tell me how I can help.

Voice: We will give you the story and you can read it for yourself.

The words began to churn and one sentence at a time the message came to me in a rhyme. I began to write and then it stopped cold.

Arael: What happened? I'm writing the story but I don't hear you anymore. The dictation stopped.

Then there was quiet. The voice had left and only a few paragraphs were written. I saved it and put it aside.The time for it to be revealed had not yet arrived. It would be nearly a year that had passed when I would discover that there was so much more that needed to come to the surface. The complexity of this story was related to a phenomenon of crossing over inter-dimensional space. I felt directed to read and study some of the incidences of the Bermuda Triangle and The Philadelphia Experiment. In both cases there were a series of strange scientific unexplained disappearances of humans and physical objects alike. What were they telling me that I needed to know or what did they want me to share with others? Is this just a matter of science being discovered or a greater understanding of those things around us? More months had elapsed and I finally received this story about Prescott, the pirate who dressed like a Patriot to disguise his true intent among the early settlers.

Prescott's Waiting...

Prescott's waiting for a sign, from the stars above that have been his guide. He followed the course by ship and sail. He traveled the seas through wind, rain and hail. It didn't matter what lesson was to be learned. He took the challenge of stealing all the gold he could hoard. There was one glitch, the wind did switch and cast him hard upon the shore. Not knowing where or what he should do he looked around for a guide or two. His men were frantic from the stormy seas and they swam in from a capsized boat through winds that created this catastrophe.

He promised his men, through thick or thin, he would share this pirate's treasure with all of them. Yet, within his heart, he could never part with the gems, the jewels, and the golden doubloons. He had many dreams in his heart and he looked long and hard as he plotted and planned to have the greatest riches throughout the land.

"What say you sir? Have you not heard, they are searching for the treasure that we never deserved," said his simple-minded deck hand. "Do you think it is safe to try to fool the King, who entrusted us with transporting his most treasured doubloons and gemstone rings."

The Spanish galleon was on it's course to take back gold from the Peruvian coast. This was a treasure prepared for the King of the Spanish army, we all know his name as Ferdinand. His wife, Isabella, held her head up high and said she would tear down every pirate's ship that went by if they stole her gold and treasured prize.

Prescott brushed off the military jacket that he stole from a ship when he lied to the English fleet's captain. Prescott said they were shipwrecked and he and his men needed a ride back to England. After a bit of a mutiny they stole off with the English ship. The Atlantic ocean couldn't contain the deceitful notion of Prescotts' wicked domain. So Prescott was off to steal another golden apple when he and his band became shipwrecked on the new land where all their treasures were worthless. You see, Prescott was an adventurous man caught up in capturing treasures from other lands; as he pounced upon every opportunity displayed, he could be called a true treasure hunter of his day.

The legends say that he fared well in any situation. A man who thinks quickly on his feet and is full of imagination. Let truth be known, when it comes to a plan, he fumbles and foils the rest of the band. He gets too nervous and doesn't think things through and in the end he gets caught and sometimes arrested as some deceitful men do.

All of these worries and all of these cares seem to accumulate until he can no longer bear it. Then arrives a few men with a patch over their eyes. Some with a crooked grin and others limping with wooden limbs. They are a rogue bunch of players, too hard to tie down. They travel the world like troubadours without the dancing around. Every coastal city knows them yet they are most inclined to stay by the mainland. "Why tarry so far in England when we can get what we need here in Boston? The ports have all that we need or want. We can hide our treasure booty right off the shore and then we may come back for more. Let's float our boat along the Cape and steal a bootleg keg or more; then swim to the lovely ladies by the shore. We have what we want or could ever need." This was the greatest group of rogues he had ever seen.

So they stayed in Boston, dressed up like good Patriots, and wandered through the city with good intentions to settle there.

"No one suspects that we are pirate rogues at best. Let's build a new ship and settle down in our new home. We can take our travels across the seas then return again without anyone suspecting a thing. They may think we are bound for West Indies trades. We can bring back other goods so they wouldn't know about our pirate ways."

They found a ship builder who had mighty ships of strength so they could sail across the ocean and hardly ever feel a wave. So they cast the sail and carried their goods and had a few flasks of absinthe and some snuff.

"Cheers! We are all on a good trip my mates!" Then the darkness began to collect by the gates. That evening grew dark as they drank heavy that night. A pitcher of gin got them all in a fight. The next morning dawn they saw the ship and climbed on. Not much damage had come to this group. Each looked at one another with a suspicious look. "You are greedy my friend I can see it in your eyes. You would take a man's life if he took a pence from your hide." Each man sized up the other and took into account whether or not he was an enemy or brother. The colonial ship was now ready to launch and it took in the wind and began to float on.

At sea it was a different tone. Prescott grew weary of the conversations that went wrong. He looked at his men and decided to speak with them about the treachery of greed and the wicked way men can be. Yet Prescott was also suspicious indeed. He had an argument with a rogue to such a degree that he brought him to a deserted island to die without food nor water or any other way he could survive.

It was a long hard trip and the men held their tongues for the fear of what Prescott was capable of. He was a hard Captain who wouldn't tolerate an upheaval and they quietly sailed to their destination in the Caribbean.

The boat began to sway in an unfortunate way when they entered the triangle set by Bermuda's bay. It began to swirl in a vortex like whirl as the ship seemed so eerie and faded in and out with strange lighting. The men were full of fright and they held on to their dear lives. An aura covered the deck as the deck hand fell from the ship. In greed he carried the gold in his mouth and choked on it while he swam. That's all we can say about him...

The hefty ship was sturdy, yet tossed about like a leaf in the wind. They all knew that something strange was happening. Prescott reached to an older sailor and grabbed him by the shirt and said, "Tell me, in all your travels have you ever seen this strange light or a ship magically disappear from your sight?"

The elder said, "No, my friend, but I've heard of this magic happening when men do wicked deeds that cause them to open the door to fatal tragedies. We are being rendered into oblivion. We are being erased from all our own consciousness. It is taking us into another dimension where we must sail until we are allowed to live again."

Then the boat disappeared into the ethers of air. Another ocean awaited them there. They seemed to fall from the sky then landed on water. Forever they sailed to a destiny unknown to them.

Then one day the Mercy of All That is Right allowed them to speak of the wickedness in their hearts.

Out of the darkness came a bright light and a voice that sounded like thunder was heard during that night.

"I could have allowed you to kill one another. Instead you are forced to live long with your brother. Learn the things that you should have known best. You must not be murdering and stealing while on my ocean's crest. It is a sacred place that sees and hears all of your disgrace. It swallows up the most wicked deeds done by those driven by their wicked needs. The only way the ocean will set you free is if you promise that you will live life more honestly."

The men began to clamor then mumbled to themselves, "We will consider your kind notions and may we be allowed to talk? We have seen many men do wickedness upon the Earth. Some of the rulers we have stolen from are now sitting on cushioned cloth. Where is their day of judgement? It is men like them who have corrupted us. They offered us good money to take what they could not.

Then the voice grew solemn, the winds around them subsided, "You will cast your sails for Poseidon for he is here to spin your pot." The voice then left and the men did sweat as they waited for another drop. A creature from the deepest ocean did take the boat with the most ferocious tempest. It was the most frightening scene as many of the men died in this nightmarish dream. Prescott held on...still waiting for a sign. Only, this time he was wondering why he didn't repent of his crime.

"It is all done. I repent of my life most holy one. Please lift me from the crime of doing all this evil. I would like to save my life if you will allow me to lift from this tempest."

The other men held onto the boat with bended knees they all wept in sorrow. "Will we ever live until tomorrow?"

One more toss and a few more fell off the ship. The harsh pull of the ships imbalance made it tip. A quick movement and the boat seemed to disappear. One looked at his own hand to see if he was still there. Then they moved into another dimension. Fifty years had passed as they stepped into a new generation. The world was so different and unusual too. The nightmare of death had ended but now they couldn't return to the life they once new. There at the triangle time slipped like sand in a glass and they never knew how they got there or how to return home at last.

Back on the seas of human existence, some sober looking pirates tore off their grin of resistance. Yet, after all this danger, a few of the pirates picked up their thoughts of defiance. A wickedness came over one pirate as he looked at the sober expression of a youthful young patriot. A hatred grew that no one else could undo and he reached in his pocket and pulled out a gun and shot this young pirate's head clear through. It caught the attention of the entire crew and he responded in an arrogant tone, "I'll be damned if he gets to begin his new life in his youth."

Another pirate remarked, "He was most innocent of us all. Why did you kill this boy when you have seen the other wicked ones fall?"

The old pirate took a deep inhale of breath then with a guttural voice revealed how his heart was still in hell. "You can change the child or the adulterous bride but you can't change the wickedness that the Pirate holds inside. Try if you dare and see if I care...You will find that my life is not meant to be repaired."

He leaned back on the wooden bench by the ships wall and showed no emotion toward anything at all.

Then the other pirates shouted out, "What a senseless death! You fool! Do you think this is to be ignored too? You were probably the one who brought us into the tempest with the rest of the wicked crew. Let's be away with you then! Back to the sea where you can be reckoned with and we will have nothing to do with you. If you have any good left in you, then godspeed you will survive the brave seas. However, If you happen to still be wicked then we have sent you back to where you ought to be. The coast is only miles away but I have strong feelings that you will return to Poseidon today."

The galley of men lunged forward and all seized him. They cast him into the blue sea and he began to swim. The ocean did not swallow him and he safely swam to the shore. In the end, it was a sea urchin who took the life from him when he stepped on the ocean's floor.

As for Prescott, he spoke to his remaining small group of pirates while they set foot on the shores pondering all their many lessons. "Wherever we may be, we should respect all men, women, land, and sea.

"...No more playing with our destiny. In the future, it will be a simple life for me."

In this story I was able to understand a deeper meaning of life, and the hidden things of the heart, the excuses for bad behavior under a guise of pointing out the behavior of others. There was quite a bit to consider. But who gave me this message? Was it the souls of spirits who had experienced this trauma? I'm not sure. The answers were never clear. Yet, I do know that this story came intertwined with something else more significant. I lived during that time period as a Patriot or Minute Man. I'm not sure completely. However, during a regression I referred to myself as a man named John Harding who lived near Sudbury, MA. Was I that man and did I know something about that ship? In my quest to find the answer, I searched online and discovered a book,' *Sailing's Strangest Moments: Extraordinary but true tales from over 900 years of sailing,*' written by a man named John Harding and somehow connected to Longfellow. I might add that the Wayside Inn, in Sudbury, MA also had a familiar feel to it despite the fact that I had not ever seen or visited that place in my current lifetime. The man named John Harding that I discovered online was a contemporary author who still lives in our generation. Interesting to see that he had collected these old tales about ships from the past. How do these synchronicities work? I thought to myself and expressed my concerns to my friends. What did I know and how was my connection to the early revolution of the United States of any value? Or maybe it wasn't. I'm not sure, but I had many interesting experiences that kept bringing me back to that time period and location where I continue to awaken to a personal reality, as I supposed was the primary reason why this was revealed. Then I considered that the primary purpose could have been to serve as a releasement or healing of our nation and the message may have been delivered by our patriotic forefathers from the past.

Getting back to the Wayside Inn, in Sudbury MA, other strange things began to happen. I had planned on visiting the Wayside Inn with my friends as I thought it might reveal something regarding my lifetime as a Patriot. Instead something else happened that was equally strange. Prior to my visit I had heard the name "Lizzy Borden," that came to me in a voice. I thought that was very strange as it appeared to be coming to me out of the blue without any other meaning. Then I heard the title of the famous old poem, "Mary Had a Little Lamb." Out of curiosity I looked online and found information about Lizzy Borden. I completely discarded the part about "Mary Had a Little Lamb." It turned out that on my visit to the Inn, I entered a small school house called, The Redstone School. This is also called the "Mary Had A Little Lamb School" because a young girl by the name of Mary Sawyer, who was believed to be the original Mary from the poem, attended that school. During our visit there, there was a brilliant storyteller who shared tales of history and legends to our group. Her poise and knowledge held us captive to her skill of storytelling. We waited in anticipation as she wove a story that bridged Mary Lamb 1764-1847, who wrote a contemporary version of Shakespeare's works called Tales From Shakespeare, to Mary Sawyer 1830, child who attended the school. The question regarded the inspiration for the poem. The name, Mary Lamb or was it Mary Sawyer, the little girl who actually brought a lamb into the classroom.

As the storyteller continued to weave her tale, the story revealed a much darker side to history. Mary Lamb was accused of murdering her mother with a kitchen knife. Mary Sawyer, who became, Mrs. Mary Tyler, ended up working in an insane asylum. During those days, workers in asylum had questionable processes and abuses with how they dealt with the mentally ill. Neither Mary was White as Snow. Their lives revealed an unsavory side of darkness that most us could not fathom.

The story teller went on to say that maybe Mary Lamb was Jack the Ripper. This is when it all came together for me. Suddenly I became aware of what the possible victims were saying from the grave, Mary Lamb was not "Jack the Ripper" but rather Lizzy Borden in another lifetime. Lizzy Borden, 1860-1927, fit the 'modis operandi' of behavior as well as concluded the voices speaking out for me to reveal this connection. The following day, I went to a flea market in Newburyport and was standing by a bunch of books. There was a woman standing across from me who said out loud, "Look, is that a picture of Lizzy Borden?" I turned around and directly above me was a picture of a woman who I believe was Lizzy Borden. Strange things like this seem to happen along the way to confirm what I need to know. It is hard to believe but this is how it all unfolds for me, and I feel that this part is somewhat complete.

I have so many memories of living in New England going back to my childhood. Since I had many personal challenges and sorrows regarding death, financial strain and other types of loss, I had longed to leave the city and had a deep desire to begin fresh and new elsewhere. This was one of the reasons why I moved to the Midwest early on. In retrospect, the Midwest was to prepare me for the lessons and experiences I would encounter back here in New England. It wasn't the memorable changing of the four seasons or the historical quaintness of many New England towns; It wasn't the ocean side views of a large coastline easily accessible to me; It wasn't my family or friends who I could easily visit from any location; It was my karma, my destiny that kept me pinned to this land to help me awaken to my personal realities. I believe I was kept here to help me to remember who I was, what I am, and where I should go. I don't think there is another place on the Earth that could have brought me to this point of ordinary and non-ordinary reality in such a succinct way. My mission, if there is one, is to search for whatever truths or fantasy that come my way. I hold open the ever revolving door of possibilities and never surrender to the times.

Chapter Eight

A Skryer Without A Stone

(A Crystal Ball Gazer Without a Crystal Ball)

METHINKS, AS THEY HAD KNOWN, I AM a skryer without a stone...

The words flooded through my head with a thick British accent and a masculine bold fervor. I was overwhelmed by the sense of power and energy that lifted my senses to a greater height. Was that my voice from a former life time? The language was archaic, yet it had the voice and flow of oratory skill commonly heard in a true dramatic performer. It sounded Shakespearian or was it Milton? Could it have been my dear friend Edgar Allen Poe? Either way, they were giving me script for what I needed to say. It sounded riddle-like, but I knew the meaning. A few times during my life psychics have told me that I have a famous writer around. I would always ask his name, assuming that it was a male from the energy I felt. Each time the intuitive would respond with a statement, "He won't say who he is."

I always thought this was strange that a writer would hide his identity, and then I thought, well, of course, the mystery of intrigue is probably one of the attributes of his personality that people loved.

After hearing multiple stories and the succession of poetic archaic prose that wasn't my typical style of writing, I saw him. It was Edgar Allen Poe. I always knew I had a dark side to me as I would glance into the windows of shadows and things not always full of beauty. I thought this was being realistic as the earth is a mix of contrasting experiences and topics. The questions about the dead and the hereafter was always around me as I could view the Earth bound souls if they chose to reveal themselves to me. Not everything was lovely and full of roses. All people experience hardship, sorrows and even untimely deaths amongst their families or friends. So, there you have it! I had a relationship with Edgar Allen Poe. I could see him in a small room sitting by a wooden desk writing. Behind him was a brown book shelf with hard cover books lined up. He had a book opened where he was writing notes that resembled a journal.

Poe: There you are! Now you can see me! We have so much to talk about and much more to write. I have more stories for you and will show you some things from our past. He held up a cotton handkerchief that had embroidery around the corners.

I peered into this dimly lit room and watched as he began to write a few notes with his pen and ink. He smiled kindly and welcomed me as if I had entered his home properly, through a doorway. I thought, where is he? Is he in a place of death where people continue to do the things they love? It didn't matter. Then he went on to say something that changed me forever.

Poe: My dear, you were my wife Virginia. Don't you remember me? I used to wipe your brow with this handkerchief when you were ill. I loved you dearly you know and still do today.

I could feel a flood of mixed emotions and I knew that the relationship was bitter-sweet. After all, he was very controversial in his writing and behavior. Yet, he was so endearing with his gentle smile and way with words. I paused and smiled...Curiosity got the best of me and I began to search online to see what this was all about. Sure enough there was a scandal of him and other women during the marriage. It was also strange that we were sort of related. Odd...

Poe: Yes, I know I hurt you but that was not my true intent. Come with me. I will show you further how we were connected.

Then I saw him in his true form. An angel at first and then fallen from grace. I could feel his remorse and disconnection from all that was good. He seemed to have mended that bridge and have come back to help me.

Arael: I understand now. Are you still in pain or have you resolved your issues with God?

Poe: Yes, I have returned back to where we began.

Arael: Am I supposed to write or is this information just for me?

Poe: It is for everyone who wants to be healed or reconnected to God. It is to show people that no matter how bad they are or what evil they may have done, that there is forgiveness available for all.

Arael: That's beautiful! I can see the love in your message. You are helping me and guiding me on my path to help others. I'm grateful and happy that you finally came forward to reveal yourself.

After discovering the connection I had with Edgar Allen Poe, I began to research his works, and there it was, the title ***Macabre*** was first his. I was directed to name my first book ***Macabre*** but wasn't sure why. I then wrote an ode to him to thank him for sharing the title of his book with me.

He bowed as a true gentleman of that generation would have done. Then he expressed his love and told me not to worry about anything and that he would be around to help and protect me. He went on to remind me that I would hear him when it was time to write again. I see him now as I am writing. He is poised and dignified, leaning up against his wooden swivel chair and his arms are crossed in a knowing way. He is confident and assured. It appears that nothing could break him. Not even the tragic life he had to bear. Everything was going the way it should go. I then became more confident and self-assured. We both smiled and said nothing more.

On another occasion, a client came by and gifted me Enochian cards, after I said he had the spirit of Enoch in him. He was a man who had a past life as an ancient King who had many wives, concubines and more. This life time took place in Ancient India where hundreds of women were gathered around him. I saw a carefully tiled floor of an ornate elegance and canopies of brilliant colors like vibrant umbrella's in rich golden yellows of Saffron threads. The sky was a rich robust blue and the woman were gilded in layers of gold and gem stones. There was an ocean of woman with rich deep brown eyes, and sun kissed bronze skin. They wore midriff tops to show their curvaceous waistlines and genie like leggings on some with long draping silk scarves strategically wrapped around their shoulders to just reveal the shoulders and neckline. The sheerness of the fabric was almost etheric. They waited for him patiently. Not a hair out of place, the glistening shine of their black hair was that of a wizards sacred silk bag filled with only the most precious of gem stones.

I was taken back by the sea of women waiting for him. Most of them were his wives. Strangely, they all looked similar, like the Stepford Wives or clones. But they couldn't be clones...not back then. It was way before recorded history and appeared to have been extracted from some ancient Hindu writings.

He asked me if I was there. I scanned the room and saw a carved open door that had ornate openings of swirling patterns. From there I was observing the sea of wives and longing to be one of them. I was there. I stayed with the virgins who waited for the opportunity to be wed to this man who seemed to have compelling magnetism that was insatiable. Woman at his feet and awaiting any type of attention. I saw myself as young and vulnerable. The other woman were hopeful but I knew the stress of pleasing all of these women would take a toll on his health and I would never know him but from a distance only.

After sharing this information with him, he sat there speechless, looking at me with such surprise and interest.

Enoch: We never knew each other then?

Arael: No, I watched you but you were too busy keeping your wives happy. You were growing older in years and had a level of contentment and satisfaction. Some of the woman were your best friends and closest confidants. You were very powerful. The land experienced peace and you had time to enjoy the fruits of your labor and the blessings that go along with it. You had many children.

Enoch: What happened to you?

Arael: I don't know. I may have grown old in the house of virgins. I don't think we were available to be taken as wives by anyone. Wait...I'm seeing something else...I see a man peering in through the screen. He is watching me. I am slightly older now and you are somewhere else. He is a relative of yours. It is one of your son's who comes and takes me and I share with him my wisdom. I have gifts that no one knows about and he keeps me safe and protected within his home. I become his wife. He doesn't have the desire to keep many wives and he is content with me. The window has now closed...

A ribbon came out of Enoch that had significance and I watched as the ribbon was loosed and returned to the higher realms. It was a time of seasons as in the ancient writings of Solomon. But I knew he wasn't Solomon. I knew he had a significant role of a deep spiritual nature. He had a wealth of spiritual knowledge that could make him one of the highest of teachers. He had a knowing about the other worlds and was so well read that one could see him as a sage. He was held back by one thing. His insatiable love for women. He knew he could not place himself in a position of power until he got control of this challenge. To my regret, I cast my eyes down and grieved for him. What a loss to the earth to have such a treasure locked up from the world. I felt that it was best that I left it alone.

Enoch: Do you know who Madame Blavatsky was?

Arael; No, but her name sounds familiar.

Enoch: She was a famous seer and you remind me of her.

I scanned my higher guides and asked them if that was one of my past lives and they said no, immediately, but you will meet her someday. You need to read about her life and learn what she had to endure. It wasn't easy to be a seer. One never has control of what they are about to see. A mere question or an opening of a door can unveil the viewing of an event that can be very upsetting at times. I also felt a strong level of persecution that she had to endure for having this gift of seeing and I knew that who ever this woman was now may be suffering from pain of rejection or had taken another road in this life time.

Arael: I wasn't Madame Blavatsky but I would like to read about her. Tell me more.

Enoch: She was from Russia and would see visions and foretell the future.

Arael: I see more of the past than the future. This is where my gift is now. I get the feeling that the future unfolds and can be changed if different decisions are made. A shifting of the time lines can change things. In one scenario we could destroy our own earth. In the same scenario, we could awaken and take an entirely different path. If I could see the future I would encourage people to prove me wrong if disaster was ahead and to shift the universal consciousness to a place where we did not have to live through that disaster in our human experience. Shift the way we think and communicate in ways that have never happened before. Rise above the lower consciousness of brutality and war and create an environment of peace. I would encourage all to see the Earth as universally whole and well. The future is in our hands to mold into a brilliance of light. If we are all awakened to our inner truths we will be able to see much more clearly and find the solutions to many of our current problems today. We have access to the greatest of wisdoms, the ability to support ourselves with food and housing issues, the ability to communicate where boundaries of varying beliefs have caused border wars. We will have access to more technological information if we have a more evolved consciousness to not use it to hurt others. We will be able to help the world and it's population with energy sources that are pure if we can let go of our miserable greed and the poison that feeds upon those who take what doesn't belong to them. The world is ours now. That means you, me or everyone, for that matter. We are in control now, but we are not all awakened to this current reality. We continue to relinquish our power of the energy of being a victim to systems instead of the reality of being empowered from on high. Our thoughts are moving floating energy that turns into matter. A solid manifestation of changed governments and of limited speeches of lies. We can call forth the truth in all matters and make the light shine upon the dark spaces of deception. We can ask that the old systems be switched to a newer system of independence and freedom.

Enoch knew what I was talking about. It was the power of intention and the magnified healing of a mass population. He just nodded his head in agreement.

Enoch: You really believe that we can change everything? I admire your beliefs and I hope it can happen just as you say. I think I am a bit skeptical about these things and cannot get myself to believe that we are able to change the systems that currently exist or that we have the power to alter the future. Is this really how you see it? I hope you are right...

Arael: This is how I see it. We are unlimited in possibilities and our younger generations are coming into the earthly plane with a sense of knowing the higher realms of reality. Some of them are very old souls and they are already coming here in a raised level of consciousness. The energy of the newer ages are now before us.The atmosphere is changing and the density of darkness is beginning to disperse. We are becoming connected to the higher source of God Energy. We are becoming who we were meant to be. The shining spark of the divine resides in all of us and we all have something individually and uniquely here to contribute to help our human cause. Those who now reside in darkness will find relief as the darkness is getting weaker and the light is growing stronger. This is not a battle between male and female power or energy. This is an opportunity for all of us to view ourselves from a higher perspective and see how many limitations we believed in and lived with, that should not have been a part of our lives. Once the chains have become loose, the true self will emerge as a glowing light. We will become victorious in the battle that dwells internally within all of us. We have been in a power struggle from life time to life time because the pressure of darkness was so prominent and overbearing. We shed this old body of darkness and reveal the truth of who we are. Many have taken on the misery of dark energies thinking that they owned attributes that led them into bondage. They will discover that it was all a lie. This is not, in fact, their true selves. This is merely an illusion of lying spirits searching to challenge the deeper workings of the inner self of human kind. When the illusion is removed we discover that we don't need to take ownership of exterior mind controlling powers and become free of the bondage it has caused many while taking them into an internal prison of self-loathing and malicious thoughts of self-destruction, hatred and isolation from the wonders of human love, peace and harmony. Many set themselves apart from the truth, they hide in the shadows of consciousness thinking they are not worthy and it was a volatile power of control that sent them into a pit of personal hell. I wish that they could set themselves free from this slew of lies from the darkest den of thieves by asking for help from the divine angels, from the christ energy, from the wise Buddha, from Shiva or Krishna, from Mohammed, from the ascended masters, from the Divine Source of all things. You can come from any belief system. There are many wise masters here to assist your path. Take back your lives and no longer forfeit your personal power anymore.

After that reading, Enoch sent me a deck of Enochian cards and a book from the 1800's about the ancient art of being a Skryer that was written by Frater. I read all the material and wrote the poem as it was dictated by the voice beyond the veil. I now knew what it meant. I didn't need to carry the burden of spiritual tools to help me to cross over the other dimensions and experience these realities. It just happened without a crystal ball, a deck of tarot cards and the mastery of skills that are taught to enhance a seers view. I was now me, uninhibited by the constraints of objects and tools. The key words came from Frater who reminded every seer that they must have a pure heart in order to do this work and for the view to be clear to the higher realms. It was a pure heart that made a difference. What is a pure heart...a heart without judgement of others, a heart willing to perceive the human existence the way the higher realms perceive it. The willingness to help those who may not accept or understand the gift. I never asked for this gift. It just opened up in my youth and I recognized the level of responsibility that came along with it. I never asked to be like someone else or asked to have another person's gifts because I always knew that each one of us has our own unique gifts to share with the world. I remember hearing a woman say, "I want to have the same gifts as so and so... an unnamed woman who was a famous speaker. I said, You cannot be her. She has her own gifts. Instead, you can share your gifts with the world." She remarked, "Oh, I never thought about that."So many people underestimate their own connection to the divine and latch on to someone else's dreams that lead them into a deeper discontentment and a loss of inner peace. Be careful what we wish for, it may come to us with a price that is far too great to repay. It is as a finely wrapped package that turns out to be empty inside. Seek the deeper rewards of being true to oneself with perfect alignment in ones path on a journey to happiness and peace.

Persephone cries from beyond Hades' sight. She refuses to stay in the darkest of night and flies back toward the sun to her beloved home and there she will be as the kingdoms do roam. No more a prisoner she flies to her birth and is risen again as the flight of a bird and sees the freedom of an unending kingdom where no one shall fall to be one of Hades' victims.

The Skryer spins into the gate and opens wide the truths for all to see. The lid now open and a scroll does drop within the hosts of angels who see. The truth now lies within our souls forever more it is there to behold and we shall rise in sheer delight to learn to rise above the fight. No need to worry. It is all stirred in good memory for the sons of light rise to remove all illusion from all that is right.

The murky waters shamed us so and we became distant from our hearts, you know. Set not upon a restful place for it is now time to take much haste. Be not content in idle words of sinning cruelties of unspoken sorts and cave not into fallen sorts but rise above the love of the war. Herein lies the truth of troubled souls for you do not challenge the voices of old that have told you your power was traded for gold and your men and woman could then be sold. It was a falsehood of the most wickedness untold for humankind has more value than anyone could know for all will be collected and pieced perfectly as a puzzle to create the greatest love that anyone could know. Still your will is open to choice. You can be very quiet or use your voice. Lift not in haste a foul word until you have taken time to see what truth is in my words.

Chapter Nine

The Money Pit

In May 2012, I was watching a television program about the ancient mysteries of extraterrestrials. I know I had watched this program before and I ended up watching the last 30 minutes of the segment over and over again. Something about the story bothered me. I knew that something needed to become unveiled. I knew that they were speaking to me to pay attention. Each time I listened to it I kept wondering how I missed some really important information previously mentioned in the program. After a while it began to click together for me. Then it happened! An ancient tablet was shown with carved triangles, domino like dots and zeros with a line through them like a symbol used in math to reflect a value less than zero. I stared at it for a moment. Some of the symbols looked familiar to me but not in a good way. I rewound the program and began to listen again. This was a place that they referred to as "The Money Pit." It was located at a place called Oak Island in Nova Scotia. There have been strange speculations about this since it was discovered by a few men who saw unexplained lights on the island and were somehow directed to stumble upon this pit. With a strong hint or lure they began digging and found this strange tablet by one of the many layers of wood and flagstone that led to a depth of over 30 feet. They were unable to reach to the bottom because it went much deeper beyond the thirty feet of layering that they could see. Apparently, this location has been a quest for many treasure hunters and notable people, such as Franklin Delanor Roosevelt. In their attempt to dig, many people have died in the process. They even tried to construct tunnels to give them access from the sides and discovered that it was a complex hydraulic system that flooded every time they attempted to advance forward by locating the bottom of the pit. Some considered that the Scots may have buried and hid some of the British Crown Jewels here. My thoughts were that it would be next to impossible, without heavy equipment to retrieve these jewels if they went to that much trouble to seal it. Some had even speculated that the Arc of the Covenant from the Old Testament, and the power that was attached to it, may explain why they had also found marks that reveal exposure to radiation that scientists had discovered. This sounds like a possibility and could be a logical assessment that something of value was hidden there. So what was the big deal? I still couldn't help but feel troubled by all of this information. My sense of mediumship began to stir and I felt there was something wrong. The tablet did not have the feeling of lost treasure but rather a proclamation of death and punishment.

I went into meditation and there it was. I saw the dead. It was the ancient dead before recorded time and not completely human or as we are today. The Island seemed uninhabited and beautiful. It all began to make sense. This was a punishment and prison for rebels. This was a place for the undead. This was not the money pit but the pit of hell we had always read about. It all sounds morbid. Why the extensive system of layers of wood and rock? Why are there hydraulics set up to flood if one attempts to enter? It is a perfect system created to keep prisoners locked in without being guarded or watched. These were some of the slave workers of the Annunaki or other very early beings who rebelled a system that they refused to belong to. They wanted to take over the power of something that didn't belong to them. Their hearts were so angry that I could still feel the venom of their souls. They were trapped in this space ethereally. The extraterrestrial lights were a reminder that some were not of a human origin. I could not prove this theory. However, I am confident that the Arc of the Covenant exists somewhere on the planet. There are probably other locations where incredible jewels and items of value are hidden. In my impression of this location, there is nothing to be found of value but rather of death in that hole and I hope that we, as human explorers will not venture down a pit that has that type of hell hidden within it. The Arc of the Covenant may be a Pandora's Box, but this is worse than illness or disease or other plague that could come. This may be an unleashing of an evil on the Earth that we could not imagine. Let the places of darkness stay dormant and let the Gods deal directly with it. This is the ashes of another world's remains contained in a well of a sinking pit and we would be wise to search for the gold within our hearts and not the magical lure of greed in spaces of the unknown. Too many of our men have died in conquests of a similar nature and found not only an early grave but may have found their souls trapped in those very places of darkness.

Chapter Ten

The Knights Templar

I never had a specific interest in this topic of the Knights Templar other than it included a sort of mystic from a hidden society. I knew that for many generations historically there have been a quest for sacred objects that retain some type of magic or power, gold and jewels. This has influenced treasure seekers, royal empires, and the like, to send warriors across both land and sea to extract, discover and pillage treasures that were talked about throughout antiquity. So many innocent people have died from the greed of others that even when the treasure seekers discovered these treasures a curse is often accompanied with the reward of wealth. Still thinking about the Arc of the Covenant from what I saw on TV and the incredible power it held. I believed that the Knights Templar not only took the Arc of the Covenant but I'm sure it still exists today.

I received a phone call one afternoon from a woman who was very interesting. She grew up in a European country and had a wonderful accident. Her voice was calm, yet commanding, as she was an accomplished business woman who had traveled quite a bit around the world.

Woman: I would like to have a regression done. Do you know how to do that?

Arael: Yes, I've been trained as a reader and past life regressionist.

Woman: Can you tell me who I was?

I reached in my bag and pulled out a card that helped me with a prayer. During my prayer I began to see in shadows and then it went into brighter light. I could see her in a past life as a woman and all dressed in black. Her eyes were intense as I felt as if she was recognizable. Could it be? There I was gazing at another but seeing, the famous Madame Blavatsky.

Woman: Tell me what you see Arael?

Arael: I know you're not going to believe this but I believe you were Madame Blavatsky in another life time.

Woman: What makes you say that?

Arael: I can see you right now. Your hair is curly and reddish-brown. You are wearing all black. Your eyes are piercing as a person who sees visions and can see into other dimensions.

Woman: That doesn't make any sense. Why is it that I can't see anything now if I could see so much before?

Arael: I'm not really sure. I don't think you were very happy with your life. It seemed to be difficult for you to see so much. Maybe more will be revealed when we do the regression. I can't promise that you will be able to see this life time during the regression. We'll open up to what your subconscious needs you to see and understand.

Woman: Sure, I will be open to whatever happens during my session.

We began the regression and I could tell she was somewhat resistant. Some people need to take control and refuse to relax and don't allow others to guide them. She tried her best to cooperate but was too focused on the results. After a little while I finally got her to relax and then it happened. She could see herself dressed in all black and described who she was. I'm not happy here and she pulled out of the regression. Immediately I was concerned because it was too abrupt for her to pull herself out. I imagine she saw something that was disturbing and didn't want to see anymore. We talked for a while to figure out and understand what actually happened in this past life and why she was having trouble viewing it.

She sat up and had a sip of water and then got comfortable on the other side of the couch. This time it was my turn to begin to see. This was not a difficult thing for me to do. I sat down in the lotus position and began to feel connected to and tapped into the Akashic records. My head felt light and the scenes began to take place. This time I saw her as a nun or a woman of Catholic devotion. I knew it was the time of the crusades as I viewed men dressed in outfit depicting the iconic red cross on white. This was the time of the knights templar. The scene opened up to one of the knights who laid on a bed bleeding from battle. By his side was a woman who cared for him.This man had an incredible gift of seeing and he knew he was close to death. Through a moment of inspiration he asked the woman to come closer to him and then he revealed that someone needed to keep the trust of what he knew. He also wanted someone else to receive the same gift of seeing as he had. Then, to my, surprise, I saw them reveal a beautiful tablet made of solid gold and the writing was in a pure black ink. The ink had a matted texture and nothing reflected off it's letters to distort the words in any way. I didn't recognize the tablet or the lettering as it seemed to be able to fit perfectly in human hands and not too heavy. The beauty of this tablet was incredible and I tried to see where it came from. The gold and black seemed like something from one of the wealthy tombs of the Pharaoh's. To my surprise, he told her this came from the Arc of the Covenant. Then he asked her to touch the tablet so she could carry the gift of foresight so she could take his place in helping the templars. As soon as she did this I knew something went wrong. She was not supposed to touch the sacred tablet and she had no control over the dreams nor was she able to properly interpret them. It was difficult because she could not stop the flow of visions for the remainder of her life.

Many life times later she became Madame Blavatsky. Here was the challenge, though she had the gift of foresight she was not originally ordained to receive this gift. This undoubtedly caused a lot of grief for her during each incarnation. Until she became Madame Blavatsky where she worked with her visions and was able to manage the information the best she could. It was difficult to view the visions at times and she never had control when they came. That life time was so difficult for her that she asked to not have to see the visions like that any more. In this life time she incarnated as a spiritual woman but not specifically as a seer. Now she understood why. She was still not fully content with the outcome but was open to the knowledge that she was fine without it.

There was a greater insight into this vision, particularly during the Crusades. The man who originally had shared the tablet with her was also of a notable origin. He later became Nostradamus.

The sacred tablets gave them tremendous insight to view the future. Although, it was a double-edged sword, Nostradamus learned to work with these visions in an entirely different organizational process. His information was constructed in a linear fashion rather than the untamed vision of a non-linear process that was hard to document and share in a sequential manner. I believe that Nostradamus was also one of the priests during the much earlier Judean time as one of the priests of the holy of holies in the book of Leviticus, Old Testament writings. He was once ordained as a high priest and had permission from God to be in the presence of the Arc of the Covenant. On a subconscious level he was very familiar with this tablet and possibly directed to connect with it so he could be prophetic in years to come when the world needed some insight. The way he organized his prophecies was in Quatrains. It was a grouping of his visions according to years, that kept a clear sense of order and description. His visions were more controlled and didn't create as much of a burden on him as on Madame Blavatsky. As a seer, I could relate to the challenges and level of responsibility I was to bear.

What I learned from this vision was to highly respect the gift of seeing and be grateful it has not taken a toll on my life as others have experienced. It may be a gift from God and we are to use it wisely and respect the wisdom that it entails. The magnitude of it's impact can be a heavier burden than the average person may be able to bear. It could be very difficult to live in the physical plane while dancing to and fro between the ethers. Quite often, as in my vision of the Civil War, they happen simultaneously during ordinary and non-ordinary reality that collides in the most explosive manner.

Chapter Eleven

Women of Power

I grew up after the woman's movement had become powerful during the late sixties and early seventies. I know it was an uphill battle for many, and I appreciate the voices and the effort of these women who stood up for a form of equally not commonly shared in the past. I didn't have any animosity toward men and I recognize that physically men are stronger and have other attributes that are here to help woman, not hurt them. With the ongoing distortions and illusions we have had to face, I am glad that a veil of disillusionment is lifting regarding this topic. We should embrace our true natures with respect and kindness. Many of our ancestors had created the divisions that we are finally beginning to see through. The gender war is something that should be put aside as we are all in this together. In my past, I know I learned these lessons and have seen the wisdom of just expressing what we know rather than trying to prove any form of dominance. After all, isn't that behavior exactly what we are trying to avoid.

As a young child, I competed with both male and females in sports. As a young lady, I realized that males have wonderful traits that can be adored and respected. As a woman, I have learned much about my respect and alliance to the many women who have inspired me. And so it goes...

Here are a few tales of female empowerment from my past that have contributed to my quest for knowledge in the area of gender. Both were past life visions as I observed one in a perspective of higher truths and knowledge, another in a rebellion of darkness and witchcraft that included the persecution of the gifts that I have now.

It began with a daydream vision...I was wearing a white dress and surrounded by women in a circle. We were dancing on a rocky pasture that overlooked a beautiful ocean. Our hair was black and skin slightly tanned from the Grecian sun. I knew that we had a camaraderie or connection that went much deeper. I began to see that I was on the Isle of Lesbos with my sisters, fellow lesbians....

I waited, the scene dissipated and that was all I knew. I thought it was strange. I could see our faces. We were healthy and the sun was almost luminous as it touched our dresses that seemed to glow. What was that? The answers didn't come to me until much later when I had a regression done.

Regressionist: Where are you now and can you tell me what you see?

Arael: I am floating over water now and flying past stone walls. It looks almost like a man made river and it is daylight. I see a soft, beige-colored stone and I am wearing a white gown and golden sandals. I think I'm in Ancient Greece.

Regressionist: Are you alone?

Arael: I think so. I feel that there are servants inside my home.

Regressionist: Are you married?

Arael: Yes

Regressionist: Do you have children?

Arael: Yes, one daughter.

Regressionist: Do you know your name?

Arael: Yes, it is Agrippina

Regressionist: Do you love your husband?

Arael: Yes, but not deeply

Regressionist: How do you feel right now?

Arael: I feel like I'm living my life without meaning. I don't understand things that are going on around me. I feel that I should understand or already know more. It is as if I had woken up from a dream and I sort of remember more about life and how the Earth was formed or information about the stars and the many topics the philosophers discuss. I want to be a part of the discussion but they don't allow me to do that here. I steal books from my husband and read them. I want to be free. I want to worship with women as they worship only with men. I believe in the female Goddesses and connect to the female energy. The women gather together and dance in circles. (This is when I realized I was viewing the lifetime on Lesbos).

We go to an Island and play on the island freely. I have lovers there... they are female.

The men do it also and they do what they want to do. We want to experience life in the same way. (Part of me felt a strong resentment about the culture as I could feel the pain of inequality that was the true meaning of my desire to rebel. I believe part of the expression of exclusive woman groups was a point of retaliation. I understood that about myself and had a strong sense of anger of how I was treated by my husband and the men around me.)

Regressionist: What is happening now

Arael: I became a ruler of the women and was respected as a wise woman. We found crystal stones and realized that they made us spiritually stronger. We talked about not needing to have wars or problems and discussed in depth about the many mysteries of the sun.

I see that my life is ending. I'm dead and there are flowers on my grave. They close the book on all my teachings. The men were frightened that the women were becoming too powerful and independent of them. These were very intelligent men or as I would say, they were "Mental Warriors." They could see beyond the cosmos and read the stars.

Spiritual beings came to visit us to help in the process. I still have this knowledge in me and I will be bringing it back to the world in this life time.

After the regression I looked up and discovered a woman named Sapho. I believe that was the life time I was living. The way I looked, dressed and the strong independence I felt is still very much a part of me as it was a signature characteristic of Sapho. I moved deeper into this reality by doing my own Akashic reading and watched tablets and parchments of information get destroyed. This also coincided with Sapho's sad ending and the legacy that was lost in print. I was encouraged by the news that I would remember much of these teachings, some of which related to a place that I called "The Land of Ambrosia."

I saw that I had the ability to take people into this place or other dimensional space ethereally and that they would experience and see this paradise. It was other worldly and highly blessed and guided by the Pleiadian seven sister stars. The visions were nothing less than breathtaking...

Today, my work is similar as I take people on journeys into the past or other dimensional realms so they can heal or enjoy an experience that triggers their memory in a positive way. I don't fully understand this work but am truly delighted to have learned this process through spiritual guidance. I'm grateful to be able to share it with others. Learning to work in this process evolves as I evolve in my understanding of what I am here for and how I can share the beauty of what I know with others.

Many years ago I had another dream that was very startling to me. It was a life time that I was persecuted as a witch. I list this under women because, historically, the Wiccan lifestyle is more common amongst woman than men. This is because woman have a specific type of intuition and tend to nurture it more than men. I have met some very powerfully male spiritual teachers, shamans, or wiccans. However, if we were to calculate the average ratio of women to men in this area of expertise, I would quickly remark that woman far outnumber men in this population.

It started off with a surreal dream. I was in a pit of water that was inside a chamber of torture. There were flat bars over my head in a criss crossed formation and four inch square spaces between the bars. The bars were hammered flat in a two inch width. The height may have been a half of an inch thick. The bars set over my head while I was in a pit filled with water to my shoulders. This was my torment! I could see people around me as they walked by and peered down to see me. I was accused of being a witch.

Then the scene changed and I was trying to swim in a deeper pit filled with water. This was a larger pit and the bars were lifted off so they could see me struggle. I don't think I was easy to kill until I gave up to the watery death that was my destiny. The people who walked past me were equally guilty of what I did. I knew this because I taught them. They had betrayed me, and I was the only one to suffer at the time.

For some reason I knew I was in France. I'm not sure where exactly. I only knew we were French. Someone suggested that this was the time of the Inquisition. It all made sense because it appeared to me that I was in a torture chamber with many types of methods to harm or inflict pain to the physical body.

The scene changed and I could feel the oppression of the governing rule of the King and religious leaders at the time. They had prohibited us from using our traditional methods of healing that they called witchcraft. We picked herbs and flowers that helped our families and friends by healing medicinally. The religious leaders of the day had suppressed the people for hundreds of years by forcing them to forget the ancient ways that kept them connected to the earth and whole. We were now being forbidden to use herbal remedies as we always known how to use and the way to heal was passed down by our ancestors. Much was being taken from us, and I had a great deal of knowledge in this area and refused to stop helping or working with others to this capacity.

I decided to create a secret group who would meet outside, away from peering eyes. There, a small group of women gathered and it began to increase. I was teaching them the craft of Earth Magic. I was teaching them what was handed down to me from my ancestors so that we could rise up and become stronger. Many women arrived and many were being taught. It felt like hundreds of women learned the craft and came to me for advice. Eventually, I learned through another reading that we would meet in a pub or local place of lodging, after hours when the usual customers had gone home. Those who persecuted us would be there during the day, getting food and drink, while we were casting spells and working magic in the same room at night.

With all dark practices and efforts of anger and revenge, we were betrayed many times over. It began with the pub owner who sold us out to the politicians and priests. Then, my own women sold me out, and I found myself in the dungeon alone while they would peer down upon me in contempt. They were left alone if they were willing to say who taught them, and they watched me die.

It was a painful life with true intents of religious freedom from spiritual persecution. Some of the women understood this more after I had died because, they in turn, also suffered from the cruel pain of death for religious freedom. It was a bittersweet event of times. Many intuitive practitioners still feel the pain of persecution and for merely being gifted with a higher sense of intuition. Life time after life time this plays out in reward or tragedy. Those who have a higher sense of intuition and insight should use it for good purposes and should be allowed to exercise these gifts freely without accusations of cruelty. This is a universal lesson that we all can learn from.

During the time I had spent researching more about this life time because I realized there was more to it than a mere mishap or another witch trial. I learned about something called the Devil's Armchair (Le Fauteuil du Biable). It was located in the town of Rennes-les-Bains. I believe we worshipped in this place and I don't remember much more than that, other than the fact that there is a matching sculpture in Rennes-le-chateau of the infamous devil they referred to as Asmodeus. He was created in the image of a Devil that was in a position, that if it was set upon the chair the devil would fit perfectly on the chair and point to a specific direction that led to other clues. I'm not sure what that is right now. That may take another day of exploration to discover what messages are left from our human history. The Egyptian Ankh clearly indicates the connection to ancient beliefs and magic or knowledge of the Ancient Egyptians and Early Atlanteans. Much of this information was forgotten and suppressed into very dark ages of consciousness.

Chapter Twelve

King Arthur and his Court

There have been times in my journey when things made sense and other times when I felt like I was in a complete world of fantasy. Typically, I am a very sensible person, a little silly or child like at times, but not that far removed from what is real and what is not. However, when gazing into dimensions there seems to be places that resemble fantasy. For example, although this may seem bizarre to most, one of the first past life regressions I had was something out of Peter Pan. It all started with a regression class. We were just going to practice the methods and technique between three students. Me, a woman from Virginia and a man from Ireland. The woman from Virginia was very assertive and determined to accomplish what she came here to receive. Her strong sense of order and take-control manner was a clear indicator of a successful practice ahead of us. The Irishman, was more of a character than I knew what to do with. The first time I talked to him in class I found myself focusing on his words because I couldn't understand a word he was saying because his accent was so heavy.

Arael: What language are speaking? Is that Gaelic?

Irishman: No, I'm speaking English. You're not.

Arael: I'm not trying to be rude but I can't understand you.

Irishman: Well maybe if you focus a little better you can figure it out.

Immediately I knew we were in for a few laughs and I continued to banter back and forth with him until we both started laughing. After a while I noticed a little leprechaun on his shoulder and I mentioned it to him. Remember, I can see into the other realms at times and there he was mimicking the whole conversation. I started laughing and I said...

Arael: Do you realize there is a leprechaun on your shoulder right now?

Irishman: So, your seeing Leprechauns now are you?

Arael: I don't believe it, first you come to me with this heavy Irish brogue and then play off like you don't believe in leprechauns.

Being the charming gentleman that he was he offered to give me the leprechaun for safe keeping.

Irishman: You can have the leprechaun but leave his gold with me!

Arael: Spoken like a real trooper!! I think I'll take both since you don't believe he is here in the first place.

Irishman: Let's talk later and he gave me a mischievous wink and went off.

At the end of our class while I was headed out the door, there he was talking to the woman from Virginia and before you know we were in the hotel room trying to figure out who would be he guinea pig and be the first one to be regressed. The woman insisted on practicing the technique of regression. I offered to be the one who will be regressed since I can almost bring myself to that deeper state of consciousness without much help. That was easy. Neither one of them was willing to go under and they were very resistant to allowing themselves to be vulnerable. The challenge is when you have two take control people in one room with only one job available. The other person would merely take dictation. I looked at both of them as they politely bickered about who would be the one to guide the regression. I finally spoke up and said, in a not so tactful way...

Arael: I think that she should do the regression because if I can't understand what you are saying now then how will I know what you are saying during a regression?

Irishman: Just put your head down on the pillow so we can get started.

Then he handed the notebook to the woman and that was that...

I was thinking, this should be fun, the last time I did a regression I saw my childhood and visited the Revolutionary War times. What adventure would appear this time. I leaned my head back on the pillow and began to relax my muscles, still being aware of their presence. I could hear his voice as if we were in an echo chamber. There wasn't any background noise and I began to flow with the experience as if I was floating on air. I was light and allowing the transport to take place.

The first scene opened up to a forest with patches of moss, and wispy filtered light. I looked to my right and there were a bunch of gnomes sitting on the rocks.

Irishman: Tell me what you are wearing for shoes

Arael: I'm barefoot.

Irishman: Are you a male or female?

Arael: I'm a boy. There are gnomes sitting on the rocks looking at me.

Irishman: There are what? What is looking at you?

Arael: There are gnomes looking at me.

Irishman: What are you wearing?

Arael: I'm wearing green pants, a green jacket and a green hat. I'm an elf.

Irishman: Really! So you are an elf now?

Arael: Yes

Arael: There is a beautiful castle up ahead of me that is all white and has blue turrets. There seems to be a heavy mist and a bog.

Irishman: What are you doing now?

Arael: There is another boy here, who looks like Peter Pan, and he is flying over to me. He is holding out his hand for me to hold on to because I don't think I know how to fly. Here we go! He is taking me on a trip and we're in the sky.

Irishman: Where is he taking you to?

Arael: We are coming to an old city with cobblestone streets. I think we are in Vienna. I see a lot of people walking by in old fashioned clothing and carrying buckets of water and other things. There are no vehicles on the street. I'm wearing short pants with a short jacket, a horizontally striped shirt, and wearing a cap.

At this time I was laughing and giggling because we were doing pranks on some of the people around us. I dumped over the water buckets and tied some peoples shoe laces together.

I laughed the whole time I was telling the story and amused by the whole experience. It was the happiest thing to watch. Then the regression took me to my early childhood.

Irishman: Where are you now?

Arael: I'm looking at the bubbles in the air. I don't think I was suppose to be here but it brought me here. There were difficult challenges on the Earth. My ears are ringing like bells. We were mischievous elves. Now I'm in a dimension of the air. It is really cool. I see bubbles close together as patterns in the air as if you could touch them and they would feel like some type of gelatin or spongy material but it feels like air. It appears to have density like matter does but doesn't feel that way. I almost think that the bubbles are more on a quantum level. As if air was magnified to a greater degree to see the structure of how it rest and holds space. It is wonderful! It is beautiful! It is creation and God at the same time.

Pause...

Irishman: Where are you now?

Arael: I went to another dimension. I think I'm in Paris and I can see the Eiffel Tower. It feels like everyone is sad and in emotional pain. This time the people can see me. They, (the elves) turned me into a little human boy so I can help the people.

Irishman: What did you look like?

Arael: I had blonde hair and I was very young... maybe seven years old or so. I would buy flowers and give them to people to make them smile.I was there to help them become happy again. The sky looked very dark and grey and there was a feeling of death throughout the country. It seemed to be in their spirit. It was very sad and I wanted to make them happy.

There's a bunch of people sitting down watching me as I try to give some milk to a cat and the cat splatters the milk all over. Then I put a goldfish on a string for the cat and they laugh some more. I am also wearing a funny looking hat. They need to laugh or something bad will happen to them. That's why the elves come to places like this to cheer them up. I'm leaving now...

Irishman: Where are you going?

Arael: I am now in Russia standing on the frozen tundra. There are other spirits here from the elements. They are the ice spirits. We are talking about the balance of the Earth and checking the water by hitting the ice with an ice pick. This is how the elves check to see how he balance of the earth is. Some people are sick

Irishman: Why are people sick?

Arael: They don't want people to be sick. They want them to heal. They want to heal the Earth and the people. The Earth and people are all connected. There is a balance that is needed to be maintained. When the Earth is sick the people get sick and then the Earth is sick again. It is perpetuating the problem of an unbalanced cycle of events. Some people have a role of helping the Earth. I am here to help the Earth.

Later I was told that I am an expression of the Earth. My lifetimes with the elementals helped me to be how I should be. My early childhood taught me many traits that I needed to do away with. It would all make more sense in time.

My third regression was even stranger. I think I haven't had another regression again because it has been so hard to believe. Yet, it was so real, vivid and extremely familiar.

The third regression had to do with King Arthur and his court. This information could not be explained unless you become open to the thought that other dimensional realms show up in a regression and can, at times, be unbelievable.

I had this regression with intentions of finding out things about my career and how to move forward. Instead, I unearthed emotions that were buried so deep inside of me and another other-dimensional experience. A wonderful woman did my regression and we exchanged our services.

Regressionist: You are in the most beautiful place right now. Can you describe that place.

Arael: I'm by the water in the woods.

Regressionist: How are you dressed?

Arael: I have feet but my skin is green right now and I'm wearing a dress that looks jagged on the bottom.

Regressionist: Are you a fairy or mermaid? Is the dress torn?

Arael: No, my dress is made of leaves. I am not a fairy or a mermaid. I live on both land and sea. I'm by the waters edge holding a fish and talking to it. They made me a seat in a tree to lie on when I want to rest or sleep.

Regressionist: What are you talking about?

Arael: We're just friends having a conversation.

Regressionist: What time in history is this?

Arael: Right after the fall. I'm very unhappy now because something bad happened.

Regressionist: Why are you here?

Arael: I'm hiding from everyone so nothing bad happens to me. Everyone is upset.

Regressionist: Why? Are you in some sort of trouble?

Arael: Yes, I did something bad and everyone got affected by it. I didn't mean to harm anyone. They are now hiding me here where I can't be found. I live with Poseidon.

Regressionist: Why are you living with Poseidon?

Arael: He is here to teach me. I need to learn a lot and I need to give the Earth time to heal and forgive me. I need to learn to forgive myself.

Regressionist: You seem very sad.

Arael: I am, It is very upsetting. I can't get past the pain but I want to heal.

Regressionist: How do you speak to Poseidon? Is it telepathic?

Arael: I speak in sounds and tones with light.

The image began to fade and a new image of a woman riding a horse appeared.

Arael: I see a woman riding on a horse. Her hair is very long and blonde. I'm falling off the horse now and I'm wearing a long red velvet dress. There are people in the forest and they frightened the horse so I would fall off. I'm in danger.

Regressionist: Where are you now? Did you get away from them?

Arael: I'm in a carriage. They took me and tied my hands behind my back. There is a man there and he's sitting on a throne.

Regressionist: Where are you right now?

Arael: Britannia. We are in his kingdom now. He wants to own me.

Regressionist: Are you beautiful?

Arael: Yes

Regressionist: Do you belong to another King?

Arael: Yes

Regressionist: How did this happen? Did you travel to his kingdom?

Arael: I was riding freely in my kingdom when they took me. He wants pleasure. He thinks I have power because the king gained power after marrying me.

Regressionist: What type of power do you have?

Arael: I have power of the Earth. The little people pray for me.

Regressionist: Do you mean dwarfs or small people?

Arael: Yes, that know I need help and they care about me.

Regressionist: Are you Guinevere?

Arael: Yes.

Regressionist: Who is the king that captured you?

Arael: Mordred..?

Regressionist: Where are you now?

Arael: I am locked in a prison cell because I rejected him. I see him entering through a door in the back of the cell through magic.

Regressionist: Who rescues you? You're husband?

Arael: Lancelot, he has the power to do magic that others don't realize. We fall in love and he gives me a ring for protection and brings me to a place in the forest where he holds me and cares for me. He is sensitive to what I've been through.

Regressionist: Do you love Arthur?

Arael: No, I respect him but I am not in love with him.

Regressionist: The people must love you very much as their Queen.

Arael: They don't understand me. There are women doing magic and blame me for things I don't do.They see the beauty of the Earth in me and they want to own it.

Arael: There's a big battle now...I'm watching it. Arthur is there. He dies and I'm laying next to him weeping...I love him now. He was a great man. The little people comfort me and they escort me into another world.

Regressionist: Where do you go?

Arael: It is in a mound called Newgrange. This is where the entrance to the subterranean realm is. I am so sad and full of grief. They try to cheer me up. They want to dance with me.

Regressionist: What does it look like there?

Arael: There is a large banquet table in the center of the room. They are dancing and playing music and tell me that one day the giants (Annunaki) will be back. There has been a lot of deception, lies and illusion. No one could see through it but me. I could have helped more people if they heard me....

I see Merlin by a big door. He has the mushroom people with him. They have poison magic. I can see a castle...it opens up and Merlin is half in and half out of the castle; between two worlds. The castle is a city that Merlin created in another realm, not of this world. I am sending a dragon to that world to break the illusion...

The spell breaks and the mushroom people turn back into the little people. That realm no longer exists now. The people now have more of a chance seeing through the illusion.

The regression continued but went into another life time entirely separate from King Arthur's court.

I had awoken from the regression with a tremendous sense of deep magical illusion. I felt as if I was in a snow globe of reality. There was this clear glass or crystal shield that made things appear not as they are. I kept thinking about the Buddha and his teachings about seeing past illusion. I thought about how our entire world presents illusions unless we open our hearts to see the truth. We are all able to lift illusion if we desire to see what is before us. By doing this we can prevent a lot of harm, hardship and injury in our lives. We can find something more real and in alignment with what the universe had intended us. I had been exposed to so much illusion that I grew sick to my stomach from all of it. It was a nauseating feeling and I can not see the purpose of magical illusion at all. It only harms human lives in the end. The magician comes up empty and his or her soul becomes barren. Nothing is gained in the world of illusion. The end result is always pain.

I had a reading for a woman and she was in love with a soldier during early Britain. He was there to protect her and all the people of the village. At this time the land was lawless and neighboring tribes were pillaging and taking what didn't belong to them. They needed a power to help bring peace throughout the land. There is more to the story and I will share with you what came through to me after the reading. It was a channeled message of what was happening during that time.

Hungry Times

The Brittons look

The time is near

The children wait with eyes of fear.

The feudal colonies were not in powerful unity so they became vulnerable to the invaders who made others suffer much punity.

A soldier waits in a full armor of mail

He stays up late to no avail

He falls asleep before the sun rises and invaders sneak in as thieves filled with surprises

Hey now, why wait to be at prey,

why hold your heavy vessels of faith and find that it is much too late.

Invaders from the North, invaders from the South, Invaders from the east and hell to pay by the oceans mouth.

No place to run

No place to hide

They have laid their sins wide open with pride.

The emptiness in faith did stir

a voice of heaven was not heard

They slept in fear almost every day and got pillaged in the most devastating ways.

The grain storehouses were robbed

Their hard labor in vain

the next harvest time they didn't have any rain.

A small group of men caused much of the pain
They were not mightier than their soldiers
They were not craftier than their wizards
They had a much deeper godlessness within them.
A young boy stands and peers at the horizon
A magnificent glow of the sun does inspire him
He has a touch of the power from within and
realizes the power from the God Source again.
He lifts his heart and hears a voice.
The lesson learned was merely a simple choice.
Connected souls from a more divine source
can provide deep protection and wisdom...of course.

He speaks now with power and inspires the adults that hour to coordinate their village to protect from neighboring Saxon, Goth, Pict who were pillaging.

The young boy turns into a leader with divine inspiration and finds insight to prevent other bands from stealing.

He unifies the villages
He makes stronger borders
He makes it more difficult to cause great disorder.

He sets soldiers at the gate so that the enemy can not penetrate and declares strategy of more that changes history like never before.

All inspired from a higher source, what is this boys name?
Why, King Arthur, of course!

Chapter Thirteen

The Internal Clock of Poetic Insight

After collecting many of the time pieces and
beautiful watches hung from many chains.
I observed them all being collected inside of my brain.
My internal organs began to chime and the gears
of a clock became all of my insides.
It ticked and tocked with spokes that wove around.
I could hear the gears churning as I turned around and my thoughts were
as clear as the most beautiful fountain of water falling to the ground.
I could gesture each motion with precision of the most detailed
decision and flowed to a poem of perfected ligaments in action.
It was smooth sounding spinning not a bundle
of metal in a noisy contraption.
This soared in my soul.
I didn't have to do as I was told.
The clock kept winding inside so I never needed to be restored.
It kept moving into space.

The times it could erase and release a new
moment to every unfinished place.
I am not a time keeper but rather a time seeker.
The levers and gears of untold many features.
It evolved or stood still.
I could travel at will and be one of the time travelers
who could learn how the universe could heal.
Take me back to the place where there was nothing but hate
and I would erase and erase the bad taste of that place.
Of the future I was told, to be not so very bold.
But to listen to Earth with pendulum of course.
See the flowing in the waves and ebbing as it stays and do
nothing else to change how the natural earth should arrange.
And what about the souls?
There are so many people, I was told, who fly to heaven
through a gate and never tarry until it's too late.
The folly of the guides, whose hearts seem open wide,
tell all of them to serve the desires of their specific word.
But The Word speaks from our hearts.
We do not need instruction as they wish to impart but to rather hear
the still small voice of The Source who has spoken from the start.
Listen...
Can you hear it ticking like a clock.
A timer beats of energy and flows right into your heart.
I love you, it ticks.
Don't fall for the deceivers tricks.
Get quiet and use your own wit to see how
everything inside you and around does fit.
Click, click the gears are now transfixed.
I am human and yet I am mixed.
The gears tell me when to switch.
I am a human yet also a clock that ticks.
Not a robot or metal that is transfixed.
No computer, no glass, no magic mirrors of the past.
It is pureness of light to keep the time just right.

Poetry of Time

There is no harm to be done only time to behold.
It is not the treasure, power or any of the gold.
It is not another way that the Universe wishes to scold.
It is merely a neutral place to find peace amongst our race and find how the beginning can never be replaced or all sinning keeps recording on a specific clocks face.
The good my friend, should never end and we shall delight to see victory in sight.
Though contrast exists, a bit of darkness still can twist, to compare the difference when conscience is misconstrued during the day or night.
This is now the time.
This is now the hour.
There is a clock ticking to ring from the clock tower.
The clock within me is not something you can see.
It is only a reminder that the truth of all life doesn't need to forever be a mystery.
You should listen to me and write this down. Your soul is turned around.
You live your life wearing a frown. There is nothing that delights you and
at all has been a burden from toe to crown.
So consider this one thought, shall we tarry
with our sorrowful thoughts or seek other ways to lift up our heavy heart.
Have Joy to share to everyone near and don't live in a bubble or
you may find yourself in trouble.
We need to be connected and the life line will be resurrected as we join into a spectacular world that has never been concocted. Oh, don't listen to the naysayers, the negative deriders, the ever-fiery fighters and the simple-minded squires. They are blinded to this truth. You may have seen it before you lost a tooth. The wisdom of your awakened eyes was not from basic human truth. There in the deepest of our heart is the ever seeing eye of the God
from above and below the tear drop blue sky.

Chapter Fourteen

Real time Time Travelers

THERE WERE TWO TIMES DURING MY JOURNEY of meditation that I had extraordinary experiences of time travel, not necessarily physically traveling to another location. It more closely resembled an opening of an etheric window to view and communicate with people from the past. I was firmly planted physically in a location in my home on both occasions. I felt that they visited me or maybe it was I who looked through the portal and I could see them or they could see me. It is all very confusing. Needless to say, the questions of 'how' always baffle me since I am not a quantum physicist or have any understanding of Einstein's theory or other theories related to the topic. Moreover, I never even read fiction books related to time travel such as the writings of Jules Verne and others. This came upon me in a very unsuspecting way. One might say that I was already doing this when they observe some of my inter-dimensional experiences. What is the difference?

They are realities and in spaces or pockets of places within other realities or a dream within a dream within a dream.

For example. I have been through quantum space. How do I know this? I felt like everything was very small. I know what you are thinking...it is the Alice in Wonderland space that we have read about. That space is not like anything else that I have seen before in my visions. This reality can be very, very strange and could be distorted, upside down, backwards or sideways.

In this space I found Lewis Carroll. At first, I didn't know who he was but recognized him. Eventually he gave me his name. The space looked surreal and had some of the colors of blue and pink cotton candy or a taffy sort of substance. It was so strange and surreal.

For a long time, I didn't think much of it until I did a regression for a client and he also described this space. It was amazingly similar how he described a purple sky, a pink terrain that glittered and blue cotton candy colors. He also said he saw people or beings that he could only see their heads. I asked if this was the quantum space and he didn't respond to my question. I also asked if Lewis Carroll, the being, was one of the faces he mentioned or if he lives in that space. The man responded with a no. It is my believe that the quantum space has different affects and views of scale and color that are not necessarily easy to define or describe. My experience with what I believe is the quantum space may not be quantum space at all but rather some other dimensional location.

The man in this regression talked about many things about our future that was promising. Maybe someday we will be ready for the messages he shared. It will help us reveal our next level of consciousness and connectedness to the Universal God or Source energy.

On another occasion, I was scheduled to do a reading and it was late evening. The moon was full and I was open to anything that came through. I comfortably sat on my bed, upright in the lotus position, awaiting the phone call from my client.

The Inter-dimensional realms have more of a surreal dream state and I will share that reality with you much later. The space of dreams or the Astral space are very interesting. There we find the remote viewers, the mediums speaking to the earth-bound souls, the fairies, elves and elementals, the ascended masters, guides, and all the sages who are here to help us on our earthly journey. We can also see the spirits of contrast, mischief and darkness in the Astral plane. There is also the subterranean plane where exists the beings of the middle earth. Maybe Jules Verne was a traveler who entered the middle earth in an adventure so he could capture the reality of a plush untouched natural space where other beings exist. Some say that this is a place where extraterrestrials hide.

I had an interaction with a client about this very topic and the phenomena of time lines crossing each other or moving in a nonlinear manner. The Toltec man I mentioned seemed to be talking to me in real-time. I could ask any question and he could answer me, unlike readings where I am observing a movie-like event and not able to speak directly to those within the Akashic records. This gave me a strong feeling that I had somehow time-traveled or entered a portal where time didn't matter and interacted with a man many years ago. Here was how I responded to a client who wanted to understand this phenomena. I tried my best to describe the event. It is difficult knowing about an experience and not understanding how it was done on a scientific level. Here is my email to her curiosity on the topic.

Hello Diana,

Yes, of course I can do a reading for your boyfriend. Sometimes a reading for each person reveals more light about your experiences. Feel free to share my email with anyone you know who is interested. They can include in the email that they are friends of yours.

Also, during our conversation, I believe that we talked briefly about time/space. Interestingly enough I came upon this statement from a Seth book called "The Nature of the Psyche," by Jane Roberts, page 8. Jane Roberts is a woman who channels a being called Seth. Your mother is familiar with this series of writings.

"The psyche, your psyche, can record and experience time backward, forward, dash -- or sideways through systems of alternate presents (intently) -- or it can maintain its own integrity in a no-time environment. The psyche is the creator of time complexes. Theoretically, the most fleeting moment of your day can be prolonged endlessly."

Here are my thoughts and personal experiences of what I have learned. During my readings I have jumped from one lifetime to another without any linear logic in regards to a basic historical timeline. At times, the way it was displayed, I have had a feeling that a lifetime in the 1600's came before the middle ages for that specific person. I cannot verify this in any way other than what I feel at the time and how the information is arranged or displayed to me. Also, I had an incident where at the close of one of my readings I saw a man who was from early history. He claimed to be from the Toltec tribe and was enquiring about the person I was reading for. He referred to her as his close friend (male) and wanted to know that he had safely arrived. Our conversation happened only a week ago but he sent this message, possibly over a thousand years ago. I was baffled... He then looked up to the sky and thanked the sun god. I had a clear image of his face which was close-up and then he turned to show me his profile. He thanked me and the conversation ended. Time/space didn't appear to exist when we are dealing with the spirit or other dimensions. There seems to be another set of rules, similar to quantum physics. Maybe they are one and the same?

I hope this information shed a little more light on the topic. However, it doesn't really answer the question but rather poses more questions. Either way, have a great night and I am glad you felt the reading was helpful.

Best wishes,

Arael

Non-linear space and the travels of other people appearing in those spaces have been baffling to me. I return to the name of George Melies, the French filmmaker from the early 1900's. His iconic cartoon of the man on the moon, who's eye gets poked out by a rocket, was at first intriguing. The memories of film school and viewing much of the Avante Garde filmmakers of the early 1900's was a delight. Their imagination and whimsical play with special effects and illusion made me smile. I could sit for hours discussing the deeper content of their complex perspective of life. They were the Houdini's of the Silver Screen. As I was reminiscing over my return to school after many years, my son was only five years old at the time and I a single mother trying to get my bachelors degree. The classroom was filled with bright-eyed students, were fifteen years younger than I was having gone from private schools directly to college. They all had dreams of Hollywood. I could only dream of survival and a local job that could put food on my table. Having a brief moment of feeling sorry for my self something happened. My inner eye began to replay a scene from a reading that I had with a woman who, in a past life was once a courtesan of Napoleon. I saw her steal his pocket watch from his jacket pocket during a ball they had attended. Soon after dancing, Napoleon then danced with Josephine and was lamenting the thought of leaving her because he needed to return to battle. He tried his hardest to avoid eye contact with the many courtesans he had lain with so to not disrupt their last few hours together. He knew that there was a possibility he may not return. The clock was ticking, but within his pocket, the sound of the ticking had subsided. As he glanced deep into Josephine's eyes savoring the passion of lovemaking they would have before his great march into war, he measured the time just perfectly when he should exit the door. He reached into his pocket and discovered his pocket watch was gone...had it fallen to the floor? He gasped, it was his life-force. Time was his key to success. He measured everything by strict calculations that were written in his psyche. The room began to spin in a dizzying way as he looked toward the floor and examined it straightaway. Then he thought of the memorized sequence of events of everything that happened that day. He could recall the last time he observed his clock and then he thought of the courtesan who may have robbed him. She was no where in sight...

The scene shifted, the courtesan stands on the street awaiting a man with white hair, a top hat, a curled up mustache, striped pants and a jacket. His eyes sparkled strangely. What did this man want? He looked as if he had everything one could imagine. She reached in her purse and handed him a pocket watch. He gave her some money, took the watch and walked away while disappearing strangely in a crowd on the street.

The scene shifted, then I saw George Melies, then I heard the name Jules Verne. I immediately went onto the internet and began looking at a web site. That was him! The man who hired the courtesan to steal Napoleon's watch. How could Jules Verne have gone back in time to do that? He was a real time-traveler. I also believed that he was George Melies. They were one and the same. Is that true? I'm not sure but that was what I saw in my vision. Why did he steal the watch? This is a question that I have not been able to solve other than I am intrigued by it all.

Then I discovered this...

Swiss watch found in 400-year-old tomb
December 17, 2008

Archeologists in China are baffled after finding a tiny Swiss watch in a 400-year-old tomb.

The watch ring was discovered as archeologists were making a documentary with two journalists from Shangsi town.

"When we tried to remove the soil wrapped around the coffin, a piece of rock suddenly dropped off and hit the ground with a metallic sound," said Jiang Yanyu, former curator of the Guangxi Autonomous Region Museum.

"We picked up the object, and found it was a ring. After removing the covering soil and examining it further, we were shocked to see it was a watch."

The time was stopped at 10:06am, and on the back was engraved the word "Swiss", reports the People's Daily.

Local experts say they are confused as they believe the tomb had been undisturbed since it was created during the Ming dynasty 400 years ago.

They have suspended the dig and are waiting for experts to arrive from Beijing and help them unravel the mystery.

I discovered this interesting archaelogical find on the internet. Whether or not this is true...I can not validate it to be accurate or fictitious.

Was the time traveler trying to tell me something? I searched further and reflected on the thought of what the Universe was trying to tell me. Someone had been searching for something. But what was it that they were searching for?

A few weeks later during a meditation session I somehow regressed back to my early childhood and saw myself in a crib as an infant. My mother came in and checked on me before I fell asleep. I got the impression it was my second Christmas. At the doorway stood an old man peaking in and smiling. His eyes sparkled. I smiled but I didn't recognize him. Now I can see he looked identical to Jules Verne.

I thought it was Santa Claus and that was very strange...

I know Jules Verne was human. However, is it possible that the higher beings come here to help us in difficult times. Why would he have stolen Napoleon's watch? Is it possible he helped intervene to protect the Earth from a fatal series of endless wars? Is it possible that Napoleon could not stop himself and an intervention was required. Could Jules Verne have been a Timekeeper. Could the watch of Napoleon's have been a vehicle to help him control time and he had wrongfully used this device? We'll never know for sure...

The story about Rupert in the book, ***Macabre***, was also an intriguing story about time travel. He was looking for his freedom from his wife who seemed to have followed him from lifetime to lifetime. Was it Karma or was it related to greater more sinister reason. Interventions from other dimensional realities can collide into our reality that can slightly or dramatically alter events in our history. How did I speak with him

He was in Middle England and dressed like Shakespeare. He had long blond hair and tired eyes, almost as if he was in a half trance state of being. He complained that his wife was constantly nagging him because he spent so much time in meditation or time traveling. She claimed he never worked or did anything around the house. Rupert told me he was the spirit who Jane Roberts channeled for the Seth Speaks series. He told me not to use the device in the portals. I was perplexed about what this device was. Later in time I think he thought I had the pocket watch that was stolen from Napoleon. Maybe he thought I was the courtesan? None of this was true and I was proven to be innocent in the questioning as he pursued his freedom from this endless revolving portal door that would ultimately free him from his miserable life much later in time.

From there I found myself talking to Buddha in a dimension of non-consuming fire. He called it the 7th dimension or 7th heaven. We had a discussion about the device and he gave it to me. It has something to do with the portals. This was not the same device Rupert was looking for but he gave me access to windows and doors of reality. I had to be able to walk through the fires of this dimension to see if my heart was pure enough to be entrusted with this device. It was not a physical object but a key that only I have or can hold. This is something that is only given to those whose hearts are pure and are responsible for the greater good of the earth. This key enables the caretaker to be able to help in all dimensional realms. I was grateful to both Rupert and Buddha for their assistance and moved on into my journey.

As for Jules Verne, he found the key he was searching for as well and the balance of the dimensional places were restored. The unclean hearts will be trapped or removed from this space and held to account for all actions taken to manipulate the higher good. He was a true timekeeper, one of the sacred wise ones who were there to protect the portal. Wizards are often held in higher esteem that what they should be. They are not necessarily evolved or ascended.Most of them, including Merlin, were humans who had access to sacred objects that enabled them to enhance their ability or power. They did not always achieve this power through a pure heart or vow to help humankind. Too often they had used their power to harm others or take what didn't belong to them.

My visit to the Wayside Inn in Sudbury MA, also revealed something interesting regarding time travelers. It was the Grist Mill that stood out on this occasion and I had such strange feelings of time travelers intervening to assist the human evolution in the area of technology.

There it was, a picture of Edison shaking the hand of Henry Ford. As I was looking at Thomas Edison I couldn't help but think that he reminded me of both George Melies and Jules Verne. What if he was the same traveler who brought us the many advanced inventions in the areas of electricity and light. What wisdom did he impart upon Henry Ford when he encouraged him to use the mills to create energy through water. As I was reading the information and looking at the strange metal gears to keep the mill working I could not help but see the similar appearance to the inner workings of a clock, as in the movie Hugo that refers to George Melies. Other innovators from our history, such as Ben Franklin, were also suspected of being assisted and referenced the concept of reincarnation. Could he have stepped through time or given the insight to higher knowledge as also a conduit to assist our process of evolution? This is just one of the many things we can ponder...

As I mentioned earlier, wizards are often held in higher esteem than what they should be. They are not necessarily evolved or ascended. Most of them, including Merlin, were merely human beings who got a hold of sacred objects and magic processes to enhance their power. It is my belief that Merlin's staff was actually the staff of Moses. I was given insight on this one day and it made perfect sense to me. How he got the staff is still a mystery. Maybe that will be revealed some time in the future if this information is necessary in helping us find our inner truth.

Many, similar to Merlin, had not achieved their power through purity and a vow to help humankind. They got their power to manipulate others and take what doesn't belong to them or were only willing to help a select group. They may often give the illusion that they are here to help everyone. The outcome usually ends in a tumultuous state of being and these people create constant loops of illusion that they can't seem to help themselves out of.

The time keepers are true divine beings and are not human in nature, though they can take on the form of a human. They are here to assist us and we should be mindful to respect their power and purpose for all our well-being. If it were not for them we would be in a constant chaos of disorder and destruction as in before time when God decided to create the earth and separated the heavens. The universe was then structured into being in a way that it should not be altered or we return to a state of chaos as written by the ancient Greek writings of Ovid and Biblical Hebrew texts. We don't aspire to rise and control things related in the universe. If we are meant to assist we will be asked to provide a role for the greater good. Let's release the egos of the past and move forward, while considering that everyone had true intrinsic value and carry a specific role that help the cause of the highest good.

Chapter Fifteen

Stories of Macabre

It was a dark rainy evening and I felt compelled to write. The sounds of poetry began to flow through my mind. Most of my stories were full of life. I channeled the words and this time I became surprised by the content. Immediately I felt the great beyond speaking endless words of tales that needed to be shared with those who were willing to listen. Little by little the collection of stories were added to a list or folder to be set aside for another rainy day. I wasn't quite clear where I would be headed but I thought, this is something very different from what I had experienced in the past. I feel happy inside. My future looks bright. Yet, these were more serious and even gruesome at times. "The Druid," "The Witches Brew," "Robots from our Future," "Underwood," were all stories of darker content, the type of story that could curl a person's toes in suspense if accompanied by the right music and mood to set a stage of ambiance. I knew this wasn't coming to my mind. This wasn't the type of fantasy writing I was accustomed to. My new writing style was poetic, yet sweet and perfect for a youthful audience.

This newer style of writing sent me to a place where darkness abounds. Yet, it helps direct the reader out of the darkness and into the light.

One of the first stories came at the least expected time when I was doing laundry. A voice of a man was heard. It was a deep, confident voice that was not very loud. He began to speak to me and tell me that he had a story for me. I could see him in my third eye. He was a man with shoulder length brown hair, deep set green or hazel eyes who was slim but very masculine and highly confident. His clothing was from a much earlier period in time. I thought, what was he doing here? A man that clearly looked like he came from England and was persistent about sharing his story with me. I thought, it was strange because typically, mediumship attracts the Earth-bound spirits that are local. This man may be visible to most mediums near his home in England. I thought, what was he doing here and why did he travel so far to tell his story? Maybe I am connected to him in another way? Is it possible that I am someone he remembers? The story, "Underwood," was about a man or a being, if I can call him that, who visits women during the day while their husband's are off working. This story lacked credibility and has elements of magic mysterious traits. I never looked deeper into the story to reveal what my personal connection was to this story or to him. I only know that he never returned again and I am content to read the story without any further attachment to it. "The Druid" and "The Witches Brew" came after an Akashic reading as did "The Land of Apples," "Jack The Ripper," and "Catherine Howard." The story about "Jack the Ripper" was very unsettling because I was not searching for this information as it came to me rather surprisingly. It was so startling that I received help from the higher beings who assisted me afterwards. I was somewhat distraught over the situation and they knew I needed help processing this. They said to me, "We will show you who Jack The Ripper was." This is an unsolved crime. My first thoughts were that no one would believe me. My second thought was that it really didn't matter. I needed to find the truth. I needed to share it with those who needed closure and the records of time only spoke the truth. I realized that this was not for gain, publicity or entertainment. This was for closure and healing of an unexplained series of murders that were very chilling and heartless. The key to the answer was in the reading. The message was that the person who was the wife of Jack The Ripper, had to work out his karma with this person in this current life time because he (the wife) had poisoned him. After the reading, I was told to look up the suspects and I would find out who he was according to what I saw and specifically looking for visuals of what the house looked like, and the poisoning that occurred. There I discovered the story of James Maybrick and his wife Florence (my client).

"The Illumined Ones" came as a vision as I watched men sell their souls for power and opened the door to extraterrestrial beings who have had visible influence on our planet through political control and big money. "The Emotionless Ones" were also influenced by extraterrestrial beings referred to as The Greys as in Area 51.

Two of the stories were about time travel. The story about "Rupert" talked about a time-traveler who I encountered during a very deep meditative state. I observed him inside his bedroom as he was seated on a bed made of straw. He looked miserable with his eyes half closed. I thought I was getting a snapshot of the past as my typical Akashic readings send me to places of the past as they are filed in a movie. This, on the other hand, was very different from a reading or a vision. I began to talk to this man in real time. I had a conversation in 2011 with a man who lived in middle England. I'm not sure I did this nor can I share the details of our conversation. The only part I understand is that he was looking for help. He was searching for an escape from his nagging, controlling wife. I said, well, you and many others are not happy with their spouses. That's understandable, however, how is it that we are talking right now? I am in your future and you are in my past. He then went on to tell me he time travels and he was looking for an escape from his wife. We didn't speak for very long but I thought, how simple would it be for him to physically leave and be with her no longer if it was that bad. Until I discovered two things. He was the one who was Seth in the Jane Roberts books. Interesting, I thought, that still didn't answer my question. At least not right away. Over a year had passed when I heard his voice again. I heard someone speak and tell me a woman's name. I said, "who are you?" He responded and said she is coming to you. So this woman called me up two months later. Immediately I knew something was wrong. My gut tightened and the intention was not for sincere help but of a darker sort. I thought, after I hung up the phone, there is something wrong with this woman. She lacks sincerity and what does she want? Then I heard the man's voice again. It was Rupert. "I want you to take the reading. Can you help me out?" "What do you need from me Rupert?" I asked. "You will see when she arrives." Little did I know that she came to my door to discredit me and discovered this to be true a few days later.

We began the reading, and as I have committed to be objective I closed my eyes to any personal issues and told her what I saw. She had recently lost a lover and was searching for him through mediumship. I saw him revealed and the eyes were very distinguishable. Then I realized that this man was Rupert. I asked, "what are you doing here?" Rupert told me that he was looking for his twin flame. A twin flame? Do you think it was her? No, it is a man. "Can you see him?" There I saw a man with brown hair who was slightly shorter than average height. Rupert said, "Please tell me who this woman is? I need to know because she is still searching for me in my death." Now awakened to who he once was and who he became in the future he began to observe her soul to track her connection to him. He was searching for his true love and was not confident it was the woman who was now asking to be connected to him in this life. I began to see the pages of time unfold. He then said, "She is the wife I am trying to get away from. This is her in my future! Why does she have such a stronghold upon me? How is she able to trap me into many lifetimes and why can't I be free? Tell her to find my twin flame and then I will be able to resolve what is happening." I proceeded to explain to this woman that she needed to find her old boyfriend (Rupert's) twin flame. The part of his essence of who he is will be with this man. This man will be very similar to him. She was delighted and relieved because the man she loved was kind to her. Instead of searching for his twin flame she went with another man with red hair out of confusion or guidance from somewhere else. I found out a few days later that Rupert was able to cut himself free from her by directing her to the wrong man. I don't know what the outcome was although it appears that he departed with a sense of contentment. What held them together for many lifetimes may have been a spell or other type of unnatural force that interfered with the natural course of karma that violated the freedom of will. Not even the highest beings would violate this spiritual law. Some type of spiritual curse or trickery was suspected and I believe the higher good assisted Rupert's soul to become free from something or someone who had violated the spiritual laws. In the end, this woman missed the connection to this man and his twin flame because her intent, though sorrowful for her loss, had ill intentions toward me from the beginning and a darkest desire to control another human being. What she hadn't considered was that she did this boldly before the higher beings of light. Nothing terrible happened other than that I am certain she will not experience any real peace and joy until she makes things right. The challenges of learning forgiveness and being objective is something that we all need to aspire to. However, I acknowledge my human side that is honest and true about what comes from my heart. A seer is not always perfect. We have the emotions and feelings of every human attribute. I don't believe anyone who claims to walk in a level of being so pure that they don't have a bad thought. I don't think this is humanly possible. I will let the Gods claim those attributes. As for me, I learn what I needed to learn and trust that there is a higher good in all my experiences that may help redirect my path to something better.

Another story from ***Macabre*** was about a group of Elves from Middle Earth. We go from Middle England to Middle Earth. This story is called "The Gotlanders." I thought this story would be for children at first. Then, the darkness and turns and twists of the plot made me feel that this might be a better fit for adults. I was somewhat amused by the story since it talked about the other beings who reside in the Earth's atmosphere and were intended to care for the Earth. Little did I know that much more would be revealed about these beings during a series of readings and the deeper nightmares attached to it. I could see them when I was writing their story. I was guided to the Island where they said they lived at one time. These were the same beings that were referred to as the Tuatha De Danaan. Unlike the typical Fae, they had an elegance and beauty quite similar to the human race. As I began to dig deeper I discovered that they were the Aryans, the beings who had guided the Nordic and Germanic Tribes. They had a strength of magic and were able to organize and etch out a land base within the northern hemisphere of the world. Despite their power there was an anger and resistance that I couldn't quite figure out. I knew they were not happy and their stoic stares into the horizon gave me a chill. They were determined to win and become steadfast in their efforts. My question to them was what is it that you are trying to win? What is your anger caused from? In the story "The Gotlander's," they gave me a snapshot of another being named Pan who had made them miserable in a form of deception and continual harassment. They get trapped into Middle Earth and cannot leave for many years. If this is true than it had happened in other dimensional realities that parallel or current existence. The question is how do other dimensional existences affect our physical plane of existence? A few years ago I had a clear vision of a man who came from Middle Earth. He resembled a long-haired Albino because he was so fair that his hair was so blonde it was white. His eyes were blue and he had a masculine muscular built. He would appear to me randomly looking at me and not saying a whole lot. I knew he was not human but was very familiar with our existence as if he had lived amongst us along with some of his people. This is how I was able to piece this story together and make all the connections. I knew he was in a lot of pain and was somehow looking to me to resolve whatever it was. I thought, "Why do these beings come to me?" I'm merely human and it is obvious that they have power. It is as if I hold a key to solving and resolving their problems." Here is the sequence of events. In 2009 I wrote the story about the Gotlanders. I had my first visitation of him during a vision in the fall of 2010. He would come to visit me many times after to just say hello and not necessarily asking for anything. His demeanor was cool and relaxed but his eyes were telling me another story in a form of telepathy.

In 2012 I had a reading that changed everything. There was a client of mine who came and asked me to help her understand her past lives and was searching for some answers. Knowing that she had a type of mischief in her I quickly realized that she was somehow connected to the Fae as a Sprite, Pixie, or one of the 'Wee Folk.' We already had a few readings done earlier and this next reading would deal with her possible connection to the famous Romanov family in Russia that got brutally murdered by the Bolshevik Party. The entire family was murdered, including Anastasia, who was believed, by some, to have somehow escaped and survived the brutal gun shots from the soldiers. In my vision, I saw the soul of Anastasia shatter like a piece of glass that fell to the floor. The shattered pieces hovered over the Earth and another woman who was living in an insane asylum became an open vessel for a soul piece that no longer had a body to fill. This woman therefore took on the identity of Anastasia as did others in a much lesser degree who opened themselves up to this severely traumatized soul who could not find the light. Anastasia did die by the hands of the soldiers and she incarnated many life times with a sense of trauma. I believe that Anastasia was also the well-known Anne Frank, the journal writer during the World War II's persecution of the Jews in Germany.

The question was, who is Anastasia and why did this happen to her soul on such a dramatic level. The mystery finally began to unravel when the reading opened up a space of reality that tied it all together. I could see in this woman's Akashic records that she was dancing very whimsically with a bunch of girls inside the castle where the royal family lived. I could see her sick younger brother who was highly anemic and didn't go outside to play very much. The impish Anastasia was a delight to her family and all who knew her. She had her challenges with her siblings as all children do but seemed quite normal. The circumstance seemed to have a feeling of a dark cloud over it. The family seemed mild and even-tempered but the atmosphere had a sense of foreboding. The tension of the Russian masses was immense as they felt discontentment and a lack of the basic essentials of life such as food and shelter. The French experienced something similar to this during the French Revolution and the starving, depleted people of France, called out for rebellion. Most governments have dealt with the curses of famine, poverty and the challenge of feeding many mouths during droughts and other natural disasters of resources. What happened here was typical of any nation unable to please and satisfy their people with the basics of life. This was understandable. However, I kept asking myself why it felt so dark and menacing above and beyond these issues.

Then the scene changed and I could see the Aryans or Gotlanders standing within a small group during a conversation. I could see what appeared to be Merlin with a small sprite or pixie. They were observing the Aryans through a dimensional portal that looked like a cloud. The pixie was directed by Merlin to enter the space unwittingly and perform a task that would prove to be disasterous to the human race. There, the small sprite or pixie who was 2 or 3 feet tall, began to dance and amuse the group of Aryan men. Beside these men was a large rock that had a crystal looking device of great importance to them. This device enabled them to travel back to their homeland since they were merely visitors on this planet. Being as powerful as they were, they never imagined that this silly childlike sprite could harm them in any way until she quickly snatched up the device and ran to Merlin who helped her escape through the portal.

The Gotlanders or Aryans became trapped in the Middle Earth plane and demanded that their device be returned. To their dismay it was kept well hidden for hundreds of years or more. The search for the device, that enabled them to travel back to their homeland, was devastating and the Aryans became embittered causing wars throughout the Earth and they tried to force Merlin to release the device back to them. It may even appear that this was Merlin's true intention, to keep the Earth in illusion and warfare so humankind will become too confused and full of problems to connect to their higher good. The Aryans searched for the device and began tracking down the whereabouts of the pixie who assisted Merlin that day. She ended up incarnating as Anastasia Romanov and they were not able to find the device around her, but their influence on the Bolsheviks created a shaking that ended with the shattering of her soul. The trauma would be connected to her soul until she resolved her other dimensional karmic issues with her incarnation as a pixie, and the theft that shook many nations. Though, she was merely a pawn in the mastermind of Merlin, she had a level of accountability that needed to be resolved. Many life times later she arrives in my life and here we are seated in my living room discussing her many challenges. I performed a soul retrieval and she became more whole. The next part of the challenge was to find the missing device. I could see the blonde-haired Aryan near me awaiting the information he had long searched for. As the story began to unravel and she clearly didn't remember any of it but could see some distinct personality traits, she sat there patiently while I observed what I could. Suddenly, in a blink of an eye I could see one of the Aryans reaching down into her hair as she sat waiting for me to talk. I watched him pluck out a small crystal, very very small as they held it between his two fingers. The device was found and they thanked me. She was relieved and set free. The nightmare was now over as the Aryans could release themselves from our Earth plane and return home. I prayed for peace that day and prayed that the Aryans would no longer influence any more wars on our planet. I prayed for Anastasia to have peace and total healing from this very old trauma.

Another piece of this story unraveled months later. The Pixie (Anastasia) who helped Merlin, was originally Niviane (Nimue or Lady of the Lake). According to another vision or guided meditation, Anastasia was awakened by a vision that revealed her connection to Avalon and the mystery of what happened between her and Merlin. She discovered that she was Nimue or Niviene or some might know her as The Lady of the Lake. Merlin was angry at Niviane because she rejected his romantic advances and he turned her into a Pixie. Merlin went on to inform her that she could not return to her original state as a Priestess unless she helped him perform this task of trickery on the Aryans. Soon after the task was complete, Niviane was returned to her original state as Priestess. However, she was too powerful in this life time, having access to many forms of illusion and easily capable of hiding her identity from the Aryans. It wouldn't be until much later in time that the Aryans discover her in the incarnation of Anastasia and the present incarnation today where she is also named Anastasia.

Merlin...he was the cause of the horrible illusion around King Arthur's court and his many followers. He destroyed the very people he raised up such as Arthur and the Knights. He was also to blame for the confusion among the British quarrels during the War of the Roses. But who was this Merlin? Was he the devil or the leader of a satanic rule? Not necessarily. There are others who have taken on roles of darkness for us to choose.

Chapter Sixteen

Legends From the Past

One day I felt highly directed to research a man named Zoroaster. There were carved stone relief of his image. A bearded man with an unusual tall strange hat and a determined look. His appearance made me shudder and I wasn't sure why. It all felt so uneasy to me as I knew I had an encounter of some sort with this man back in time. The feeling was that of distress and anxiety. The feeling was the helplessness that one might feel around a dictator. The uneasiness that still remained reminded me that I was probably badly mistreated or observed others being mistreated somehow. The emotions began to stir and I didn't have any words. Suddenly I began to see out into a vision and hear this...

Off in a distance I heard comforting words... "Come my little one, come play in the fields and worry not of the sorrows and pain." There I see an old gentleman, sort of grandfather like but not anyone that I remember. He calls me out to comfort me now in my memory of pain. I see the field and I am transported as a child playing and running after butterflies. The grasses are much higher and they are near my waist. I see tall purple lavender floating amongst the tall grasses. The sun is out and the magical field begins to ease my pain. I feel the love of God and I reach up my arms for his embrace as he speaks to me gently in whispers of comfort. Then I am seated by a tree as a beautiful white horse watches over me. This is the place where angels breathe and delight and retreat from the cold harsh cruelties of the world. This is the place where God's love is pure and nothing can intrude or taint the very essence of truth. The light is bright but soft upon the skin and the plants are not visually sharp but have a gossamer like trim. I lift my soul to peacefulness now. "Rest and sleep under the tree," he says to me now. I lay in a cushion of soft grass and rest in the most beautiful light of day. His beard is like white cotton and so pure. His eyes are like diamonds of shades of blues and grays as the sky does change within in many types of ways. "I love you" he speaks and says nothing more. I am content to be quiet and search through his eyes for more. "I love you too," then the quietness is lifted again he reaches across to me and touches my forehead. "Be healed and be free the way you were meant to be." I feel an inner peace and I lay my head down to sleep and he is still there in my dreams like a father who guards his little child by the trees.

After this beautiful moment in time I relaxed and slept. My dreams were absent and a slight trembling of energy flooded my soul. I woke up refreshed and felt the lightness of the morning sunrise. The sounds of cars drove by and I am startled by an alarm. I get my son ready for school. It is time to get going and we make coffee and have breakfast. The TV is now blaring and I look at the time. We jump in the car. Now the music is blaring to wake up our tired eyes and find energy from the beats of the music and harmony of contemporary sounds. The electronic waves awaken my son in between his studying and memorization for one of his many tests and papers due at Catholic School. He eats a bowl of cereal in the car and balances it slightly by the arm rest, not quite fitting where the drinks cups should be. I see the milk toss to and fro as we turn at green lights in heavy trafficked streets during rush hour. It is a long road but filled with all types of people. I wear my hair back comfortably with yoga pants and t-shirt. He wears a High School team baseball hat, khaki pants, Sperry boat shoes, and an oxford shirt with a t-shirt peaking through the top. He is ready for whatever the day brings. The baseball bag and equipment sit in the back and backpack full of books, notes and a heavily marked-up schedule book. We stop and exchange a few quick words with a sharp glance and grin, he puts the bags over his shoulder and is off to engage the world.

I settle back in and carefully drive from the campus, cautiously aware of students weaving in and out of the roads in their attempt to get to class. Some are crisp in view and others disheveled a bit with prep-school-Kennedy-hair and a tail from their shirt slightly hanging out in the back.

Merging with traffic has the dog-eat-dog flavor of life. We wouldn't know anything else here in New England. It is something that once you experience it, you never forget it. It can't be compared to the glitz and glamor of New York City's flashing lights. It is more sensible, traditional, and conservative...just the way we like it! We make no excuse for our city and landscape. Our earliest national history proudly states that we don't want it to be altered one bit. I see the trees along the sides of the road and laugh about my friends reference to another small highway that reminded him of Sherwood Forest. We take the good and the bad. The good makes us smile and the bad of our surroundings allows us to exercise our opportunity to sharpen our wit with sarcasm.

I'm reminded that I live in two worlds. Not intentionally, it just happened similar to someone bumping into a person on the streets. The moment is casual, we turn for one moment and there we are in a head on collision or nearly bumping into a stranger walking in the opposite direction as we are equally distracted by all the activity around us. This is my life...I never searched for the answers. They came to me in all different directions or for unexpected reasons. I never thought that it was possible that by not processing, over thinking or searching for a star to drop from the sky, I could discover or realize some amazing things. The trip home can get very involved with thoughts of what had just happened, and during that time something else is happening. The information doesn't always come in at the most convenient times. Quite often I am driving and I hear myself think, "Oh yes, I need to write that down." This is obviously not the perfect time to take notes while driving a car. Then there is an overwhelming amount of phone calls and people who want to talk for hours. Or is it me who wants to talk for hours? They ask me a question and it's a stream of information. If it happens I'm channeling their answers and they are perfectly content, happy and thank me for my time. My life can be very spontaneous and scheduled simultaneously. I guess I allowed it to be that way. I don't know anything else and I have concluded that I may be wired that way. The phone calls and streams of informations sometimes come in at the same time. Do you think the higher beings realize that their time is somehow colliding with my time or do they have to eat and run, and before we go, you need to write 3 more paragraphs in the next story regarding...such and such. By the way, John Doe will be calling you and we want you to pay attention to his reading because this will be pivotal in his business decision this week. Make sure you tell everyone about this piece of information in your next newsletter. Don't forget to call Mary and tell her that what you saw in meditation today, and the list goes on and on.

Then I realize that my thoughts are elsewhere and I missed my turn. Ok, time to turn on Sean, my GPS, who guides me so I don't have to think about where I am going. Some people find it amusing that I am intuitive but I can't find my way home if I don't plug in the gps. I leave a building and have to think about which way I came in. The Universe did not equip me with a natural compass. As a child I was such a daydreamer that they called me a space shot. Today, people think it is amazing that my head is in the clouds because it actually serves a purpose or has some beneficial aspects to it. Not everyone is wired the same way. Historically, Intuitive in the past were highly persecuted.

I had a clear vision of a past life during the Witch Trials of the Inquisition. I was trying to stay afloat in pit filled with water inside of a large torture chamber filled with accused heretics and witches. The criss crossed, flat-faced metal slatting rested on top of the pit where I had possibly 2-3 feet of room beneath the floor level to extract air. I reached for the bars to allow me to rest. I, amongst many intuitives at the time, was brutally persecuted. I never saw myself die in this vision, but I am grateful that the grace of God only reminds us of our lessons to learn not to cause us any deeper pain of remembrance that isn' t necessary.

More recently I came to realize and remember two other lifetimes where I was persecuted for my gift of second sight. I was in America's Stonehenge in Salem, NH. This is a series of stone structures used to mark the equinoxes and solstices, whereby qualifying it to be called a stonehenge, though it does not have a similar appearance to England's Stonehenge. There I was, walking through the ancient structures and I had a strange feeling of familiarity. I started sensing that this was not a place of ancient native people but a group of settlers of Caucasian descent. I didn't watch the pre-movie because of my enthusiasm to step right out into the space but I did begin to read the written material that had a descriptive map. That was a large stone slab that was referred to an altar. It didn't feel right to me and I ignored that area. The startling part was my entrance into each cave. It was amazing. They were filled with emotion and secrets from the past. I could feel the energy of antiquity bubbling up and the presence of native people whose souls have had not departed and settled here after the Caucasians were destroyed…that was my feeling. The most memorable part was when I stepped into The Oracle Chamber and felt directed to look up to the ceiling of the chamber. Something strange happened, I could see right through the chamber up into the stars. What made this even more unusual was that it there was bright daylight outside. I was a bit startled and didn't expect this to happen and I observed through my third eye to see why this happen. There I saw an old woman with pure white hair in a meditative trance. It was me gaining insight for the people of the tribe. I looked up and could read the stars and weather and other things happening that would assist our survival. It is important to realize that they didn't have access to the weather channel or newscasts that informed people of impending danger. The seer was important to our ancient tribes. The seer was appreciated for his/her gifts and their contribution to the well being of others. I realize that not all seers are perfect or have the best interest in mind for everyone. Some use his/her gifts to help others. Some use his/her gifts to help themselves and some do both. Unfortunately, some use his/her gifts to hurt others. This, however, never makes the gift good or bad. It is similar to having a keen math mind, some use it for calculating and contributing to society, others use this ability to steal or manipulate others. We all contribute something of value that benefits our world. Some choose to use their gifts and some don't. Free will has always been a factor in all of this.

Well, the short story made long…another tribe wanted to overtake our tribe and was unable to permeate or surprise us unexpectedly. Until, one day, they realized that I was the oracle or seer and targeted me for death.

Soon after my death the tribe was overrun and destroyed. It must have been my time to go. To all things there is a beginning and an end.

Another vision came to me during an ancient time prior to one of the floods. Science has shown that there was more than one flood that occurred during our history and not necessarily the life time of Noah. I was a priestess and Oracle for the people. Our tribe was ancient, wise and rugged. They had endured many battles of beings on the Earth and may have been chronicled in Ovid which writes of ancient Greece or the recorded lineage of the Greek people.

I stood there in a long garment. My hair was pulled up and dark in brunette soft curls and waves of a loose bun with strands of curls hanging down. My garment was white and gold clasps held the sleeves up on my shoulder. My skin was slightly tanned and my eyes were a deep purple blue. There were many people around us and involved in our belief system and connection to the Earth. No one could permeate our system. There were the Nephilim who challenged us often.They were the giants of the land and part Annunaki from the mixing of Gods and men. Still, our energy was at a height that they could not overtake us despite there enormous strength and physical power. They could not match us spiritually because they were not pure in heart and did not have favor with the higher realms.

However, there was one challenge that I could not face. It was our leader. He was a man of strength and valor. None dared speak to him without respect. His personal power was so great that he would rule the group to an extent that at times proved to be detrimental. His self-serving attitude required all women in the tribe to provide him pleasure. The men were all at his beck and call whenever they were to go into battle or when he decided that he wanted them to celebrate. None dared to not show up with the fear that he may accuse them of not being a part of the group. Some were even cut off for the slightest disagreement. He wouldn't murder or torture anyone. He would ex-communicate them and have them try to survive in the dessert or the wilderness alone. Many survived but didn't dare attack him later. Most recognized that he spared their lives and could have been a more severe dictator than he was.

His eyes were intense and hard to stare down. They were so dark brown that they almost appeared black at times and he could be seen staring from across a large room or space. At times his eyes would sparkle like black diamonds. He was bald or had shaven his head. There wasn't any facial hair other than strong black eyebrows. His body was average weight, muscular and of a medium height. He wore a roman like cloak about his shoulders in a deep red color. His arms were bare, tanned and markings on it that appeared to be dirt. His face also seemed to have streaks of dirt on it or uneven markings around and on his head. I later realized he had the mark of Cain, as described in the Bible. It appeared as dirt but may have been black or ash colored burn marks as if he was struck by a bolt of lightning that left permanent markings going downward and in a lightning-like behavior. He had an ability to entice and seduce large masses. But he didn't, or he didn't want to at the time. He was only interested in our group. We had a higher purpose that only he and I knew about. It was to help keep the space of the Earth safe from uncontrolled powers or invading armies of entities from other extra-terrestrial places. He had the power to control. I had the power to see in all ways and places of realities. I could see the entities enter into local tribes and help them rise up against us. We would do battle in spirit at first to disarm them. Then the small army would take them down. Finally, one of the beings who challenged us realized that we were working as a team and sent a seducer to him. She was a woman of average beauty. Had she been of extraordinary beauty he would have been suspicious. She arrived out of nowhere and was welcomed by the group. I felt concerned but he told me she was lost in the dessert and needed assistance. There was nothing to worry about since she was harmless.

Like all women who were a part of the tribe, she became his lover and began to integrate his mind. The power, control and violence reached a peak not seen before. She or he, it is hard to decipher what this being was, had permeated his mind to the violence and destruction she held inside her. Nothing could stop the hatred for not only our tribe but for all humankind. The universe began to rumble as the guardians began to stumble. We could no longer hold the power because a great evil had permeated our system. The concern about a flood kept coming to me in my dreams. The ruler developed a tremendous hatred for me while he was being manipulated by a force of unseen strength and wickedness. His desire for power and women made him vulnerable to this challenge.

I saw myself approaching him to tell him about the floods and feeling relieved that he still respected my insight, despite the fact that he had a seething hatred for me. Humbled, I kept my voice low and submissive to not stir him in a contrary way. Nothing worked to persuade him that I was not his enemy. Finally he approached me one day in front of the tribe and said that we are all moving to higher ground because of a flood that would be coming soon. "Now let's prepare for our departure," as his eyes were fixed deeply into mine. Not moving a muscle, he leaned in closer and I knew that I shouldn't move. "Everyone! Gather your belongings and let us prepare for our journey or exodus to the mountains…except for you." He whispered the last statement as his eyes seemed to reach out and pierce my soul.

The tribe gathered their belongings in wool blankets and placed them on the beasts of burden. Food stores were wrapped for travel along with small amounts of water. We didn't have lot of treasures or statues. None of that was necessary or a part of our existence. There were not many children. The leader could not bear children and it was suspected that he was not of human origin. Nor could I but I do believe my biology was more organic. The few children belonged to some of the others in the tribe. They began to exit and I stood there alone weeping, no one dared look back. He grabbed the arm of the woman who had deceived us and walked close to her assuming she could take my role as the oracle.

Overcome with sorrow and abandonment I was entreated by a wandering tribe of Jews who allowed me to stay with them. I warned them of my vision and they respected my ability to foresee. They asked what we should do and I searched the higher realms for answers and was delighted that they had not abandoned me as well. This was the higher order of things for the Jews had been selected to be the high guardians on the Earth in replacement of my former tribe of unknown origin to me now. I had a clear vision of a cave that had a unique natural tunnel system and we all went there for protection. Having prepared ourselves with food and warm protection we did not realize the wisdom involved.

I lived peacefully with these people and felt love, acceptance, and appreciation as if I were their family or people.

A cataclysmic event took place that shook the earth. We got hit by a meteor that shifted the poles just enough that it brought us into an ice age. The warmth of inner earth protected us in the cave. The flooding and freezing began to happen and in the mountains where my tribe fled to, they were instantly frozen after escaping flooding waters. Their bodies turned to ice and encapsulated them into a frozen death. The man, the leader, would later become Napoleon. Returning in power he found his own defeat from an abuse of gifts that should have been humbled him and should have been used for a higher good and not for war or anger.

The Jewish people or Hebrews had pure love. They had a true sense of family, a understanding about the value of life and were humbled knowing of their humanity. God smiled upon them and helped them since their hearts were good despite the corruption of many tribes around them. They didn't spend their lives plotting wars or creating defenses. Instead, they were farmers, herders who loved their families and people. At that time, they were not of a priestly order so God sent priests to them to help them raise within the dominions.

If I were to speak about the stars some may say that I am foolish and not in touch with reality. In many cultures we hear about extraterrestrial intervention. The Dogon Tribe of Africa claims Sirius as their home as do the ancient Egyptians. The Mayans claim their connection to the Pleaidian stars. In my vision, I saw the Jewish high priests come from two regions of the galaxy. The first was Pluto, these were men and only men who had almost dread-like braids with strands of colored material throughout. They wore a white hat that protected the top of their heads and white robes. They had some type of mala beads before the ancient Tibetans. Their skin was fair and luminous. Their eyes were typically green or grey and their hair was brown. None of them had red or blonde hair. They used the six pointed star or star tetrahedron and the flower of life as an emblem. They were the ones who originally shared the concept of the merkabah to the rest of the Earth. They had wafers of life, possibly the manna? They also introduced metallurgic teachings and osmosis or acute scientific methods of transforming matter. They created a geometric barrier that helped preserve the Earth from harsh galactic intruding elements, meteors or spores and other matter that could be harmful to life on earth. They knew how to prevent the climactic imbalance as it happened before, I mentioned this previously, when we fled into the caves.

The second group of priests were the People of the Sun. They looked Mayan, Asian, Ancient Egyptian or even Atlanteans (we'll get into that later). Their hair was black and had bangs with bluntly cut hair below their ears like the Mayan tribes. They had brown or blue eyes. Their skin could be tan or yellow (Asian). Originally they were a culture of men who had evolved into having females as a part of their race. They wore white robes and two sashes crisscrossed across their chest. On the bottom of their robe they had some type of tassels and I noticed they had bare feet. They looked very similar to the ancient Levitical priests drawn during the time of Moses who protected the Arc of the Covenant. They had a purity of healing through sounds, tones and instruments. They could heal the water, air and earth. Both groups arrived to be as pillars of the Earth. This was prior to the time of the Arc of the Covenant. They carried the Holy of Holies within them. These beings were of pure light and helped the Earth immensely and they carried the energy of the Holy of Holies within them. They were devout priests and held the energy in place for many years. After many generations of existence they began to integrate with the human population, having families and exposing themselves to a lower level of consciousness. The priests could no longer carry this light and they were instructed to prepare a place where the Holy of Holies would be. This was included in the book of Leviticus to help assist and inform the priests how to care for and retain the incredible pure light energy that was to assist the Earth's natural and metaphysical world. I don't agree that it is a Pandora's Box as some may believe. If we are exposed to the energy of the level of purity of God we will die because our bodies or souls are not pure enough. A Pandora's Box seems to be a lifting of a box filled with hardships and curses. I suppose it could be possible that a violation of the purity of God's light could have repercussions that one might not want to experience. The Bible does refer to the curses that were sent to Pharaoh while they had the Hebrew people in exile and Revelation also refers to a list of fatal happenings to those who do not turn their hearts to God. That also has a Pandora's Box list of hardships. I will leave the rest of this alone...I only know what I see as an observer or seer. You can take what I see with a grain of salt or research to find if there is truth in any of it at all.

The entrance of the Priests was the grace of God to help preserve and protect all human, plant and animal life. There have been many other interventions to assist us. Some we know about and some we don't realize even happened because they occur on other dimensional realms. As it is above...so it is below.

One of the first falls occurred after the priests had amalgamated too much into human societies and integrated their seed into the human race. The information I received about the Arc of the Covenant was that it came directly from the Annunaki and the planet Nibiru. There were distinct instructions that no human should touch within. The fabric of the lining had metals not indigenous to our planet. When our society raises it's conscious high enough they will be allowed to see and learn more about the mysteries of the Divine Beings and ancient practices.

We have been consistently receiving good energy from the Sun's life force to the Earth for thousand of years. However, this was not enough to help the Earth in it's many different natural challenges or needs.

The alternative to this problem was a group of beings who were indigenous to oceans and were helpful in keeping the atmosphere pure. The Lemurians were water beings essentially etheric and kept light particles in their form. They existed on the Earth to fill in the space which the pre-Judean priests struggled to do. This is not to say that one was greater than the other. Since the Lemurian body was etheric by nature, they were not challenged with the physical temptations as the pre-Judean priests were.

The legend of Lemuria or Ancient Mu, was written about long ago. I have journeyed to Lemuria in visions and dreams and through readings. I will not go too far in depth on this topic but rather discuss that it is the most beautiful, plush, jungle-like region I have ever seen. The landscape would rival any tropical island on the Pacific coast. It may have been closer in fauna to Madagascar. I found a clearing with a river running through it, that looked nearly identical to what I saw in my vision. The thick dense jungle surrounding a stream of beautiful clear water for bathing and drinking because it was always flowing. The rocks on the edges were perfect for sitting on and it also allowed for a gathering hole for many. Tucked into the middle of dense jungle it felt safe and free as if one was nestled in the arms of their mother. A few years later I did a regression and Lemuria came up. When

I asked the location where Lemuria is now, I was told Africa. Since the continents have shifted and the tectonic plates have changed our location has changed a bit. It may be possible that this land was closer to the Pacific at one time? I'm not sure. What I do know is that I moved around the Island a bit. I wasn't located in one specific place. I knew the rulers and respected how things were run. I observed myself walking along a path where there were tree covered mountains surrounding us. I also had a strong sense that this was the place of Eden, written about in the Bible. Is it possible that the Garden of Eden existed here? I'm not sure. I only know what I feel and sense when I am presented with unexplained visions of the past or other dimensional realities. I typically don't ask to see something. In most cases, I have a vision and then ask where I am and why am I seeing this now. There are times that I have been told to journal and archive the experience or insight I receive so I can share with others. There are times that I am asked to learn something about my own life by the message. Another time I did a reading and saw a beautiful wedding performed on Lemuria of a woman who had a past life there. Here is what I saw...

I saw two ceremonies during my vision.

1. One was a wedding. In saw a couple and each were holding a 2 foot stick in their hands. They joined the sticks together to ignite them. I was told, it was to symbolize that they were twin flames. Then, I saw them standing in front of the priest. The Bride was wearing a long tunic to her feet and then there was a shawl that went over one shoulder and maybe tied or secured at her hip where it intersected. It was in all white cotton or linen type of material. The groom was wearing a toga type of outfit to the knees. Interestingly enough, the bride wore sandals and the groom was barefoot.

2. The second ceremony I saw the woman as a spiritual leader in her village. She seemed to be tall, lean and blonde. The rest of the tribe were smaller in stature, also lean with black straight hair, similar to Egyptian or the Mayan people.

The woman created a circle and set up a group of stalagmites she took from a cave and carefully placed them upright like you would when making a campfire. She had two pieces of crystal that were facet cut. One was a ball type of crystal that had a diamond cut on all sides. The other was a cross that was equally sided and 2-3 inches thick. The woman held one of the sides of the cross in her right hand and held it horizontally over the stalagmites as the sun seemed to be magnified through the crystal. I am assuming that this was a process to start a fire. Yet, the center never appeared to be lit while I observed the process. She then placed the crystal cross into the sand, near the waters edge, as if it were a tombstone. Then to the left of the cross she placed 3 peacock feathers. To the right she placed 3 oranges. I was told that this would stay in place for 7-10 days. Within that time I saw a rather large bird appear that I wanted to call the Bird of Paradise or Thunderbird. I knew it was multicolored but I didn't see it clearly. It took all three oranges. Then I understood that this was a prayer request to the Sun god. If the bird appeared and took the oranges then the prayer would be answered. If not, then it was rejected.

Later in the reading I saw a volcanic reaction to the city. I could hear the waves of the ocean as I noticed that many people were floating on top of the Pacific Ocean due to the volcanic ash. I could hear voices of anguish. The skies turned black and I remember the anxiety of those who survived having to hear the others die slowly. The visibility made it impossible to rescue others. The cries came from the dark ocean and it was too dangerous to travel back in. I didn't see this...the bodies rotted on top of the surface of the water. I had a quick glimpse of skin dried tightly over the skeletons. It was horrific.

I also saw that I lived there during that time and survived. I saw a city and people who I knew were governing the city or entire continent?

With the fall of Lemuria others fled to Atlantis. Some people believe they existed during the same time. I believe that many were the same people at first who decided to find another land that could fulfill the needs of the people. I believe that some of the Lemurians chose to step over from the etheric realm and into the physical. They traveled across Asia and stopped at Stonehenge to call upon The Powers to assist them. They could build and move large objects from their mind. Lifting great weights with only their eyes. I believe I was one who could do that. I felt a power within me and then the objects moved. I could form matter to create other things as well. When we opened a portal in Stonehenge we embarked on creating our new land. Little did we know that by opening the portal to assist us in starting our new land that we would allow entrance of other beings who could now access our planet.

As a high priestess I could help hold the space of the Atlantis and would stand on top of a high, crystal-mirrored building that had the face of a pyramid with gold and green from the blue sky, sun, and the green earth.

I saw myself moving my hands in a motion to clear the atmosphere and matter. We were capable of moving matter and creating building structures from the building blocks of life. We did this with our eyes, mind, and energy. We could build and move anything we imagined.

My appearance was dark-haired and tan skin. My hair was cut very much like an Egyptian. I looked like an Egyptian. My eyes were blue and I wore a long, white garment.

In my inner ear I began to hear a story about the beginning of my time. The mystical voice was maternal, helping me through many difficult times in the past. I knew this voice as it came to me so comforting and I nestled on my couch with a blanket and pillow and began to fade in and out of sleep. The story came like a surreal dream. Whether or not it had any truth...it didn't matter much because it brought me to a place of serenity. Before it all began she told me her name, Arano.

> *"Way back in time when amphibian beasts roamed the Earth, you were incarnated. That's how far back you have existed. There were many long lifetimes filled with many challenges, more than most humans who are now alive. One of your earliest incarnations was on Alpha Centauri, beyond the sun, in a star system unknown to humans. With a body with scales, similar to a fish or as sleek as a fish, curvaceous and feminine as sort of a mermaid-like creature. Your consciousness was highly connected to the amphibian-like creatures such as whales and dolphins. Though you no longer live near water, you are still close to the ocean enough to breath in its essence that fills your life"*

A scene of ocean blue water with high towers of buildings and castle-like structures filled my mind. The beings were many all encapsulated beneath a watery like substance unlike the ocean of earth. I could feel the density of the substance and yet move freely through it. The water appeared similar to the strange particles and bubbles in the Air that I remembered from my childhood again. It was beginning to make sense. I still remembered the environment that I once lived in, a thick dense substance with bubbles and other artifacts of lines and geometric structures when I stood apart from it. While I was in it my vision was perfectly clear, almost crystal clear and I could see as if I was floating within a magnified lens of glasses that brought into focus every hairline detail around me. The depth of field could be altered to draw certain items in to clearer view.

"You were forced from the water years ago and a great judgement of those who caused this problem will come to pass."

I saw a darkness fill the sky above the water table as black beings with wings and bodies of amphibians but hostile, not like the soft blues, purples, grays and greens of our people, hovered over us. In a dense cloud millions of beings were there to close the outside light above us. We were blinded by the darkness as other troupes of these beings began to enter our untainted waters. They had a vision accustomed to the darkness of inner life, buried deep in the central burrows of planets to accost all purity and strip it from its very formation. They plotted to overthrow all those beautiful creatures who carried the God Source light from within. They, the beings who chose not to flow in the light, became blackened by their own hatred. The only unifying force was a being, a beast, most hated and despised. It's form seemed rigid at times and then flowed like a garment whipping in the wind, a black sheet of rippling powder that floated downward to release the death of all that was good. This is how many of the planets were destroyed. They stripped the planets of resources and vital minerals, waters, and other life-sustaining elements and products to disarm all unsuspecting gentle beings. This is how they were eliminated in mass quantities. Many beings fled to Earth as a safe haven to rest. The Earth was originally seeded with all beings. All things are alive. The plants are living things, all manner of beast of the field, humans and other beings that originally came here integrated with human life.

"Because of your age and length of incarnations we realize that there are too many to peel away. You will receive full restoration by being obedient to the information of the Five Channels of Energy."

My mind began to race…The Five Channels of Energy. Who was that? As soon as I began to ponder the thought, it came to me…The Blue Moon. It was the Pleiadian lights the mystical beings I saw that visited me while I was in a trance. The four female beings who were pure white in skin tone and a soft white glow about them. They were wearing white Grecian-type gowns that looked like a dress of a woman. Their egg shaped heads were bald and the chins came to a point. Their eyes were like deer, big and brown as a knowing doe. Their mouths, ears and noses were very small. They telepathically spoke to me for over 20 minutes. During that time I saw a round, white temple or room. The top was open revealing the dark evening sky and star lit constellations. The Pleiadian women stood in a circle holding hands. From the top of the opening there descended a white globe that floated down and gently landed in the center of the circle. Then the queen of the Pleiadians emerged from the globe. The scene shifted to a group of beings that I had witnessed in a room with my guides. They were a galactic council from Orion. I don't know if this was the Five Channels she was speaking about but it was beginning to make sense. Many other beings visited me briefly, including the Greys who had come to me upset about the way we were running our Governments. They were aware that I had no say in the matter. I know that many people have been afraid of them. I have not had any problems. They are working with the issues of not having the same emotional makeup as we have. They can be perceived as being quite cold emotionally. I will say that they played with me, as if I was a child. I recall a time when I said, very loudly in my mind, "Wow! They look really strange." Their response to me was a quick image of my eyelashes from a profile, and then saying, "you look like a bug." I had to laugh, they also found me quite amusing and I couldn't help but smile thinking about it. I began to tune into the message to hear Arano again…

"The Five Channels of Energy are called the Origin by some. They existed for so long that no one knows how old they are. You have worked with them in the past, in other lifetimes and dimensions. Though you visited the Pleiades and Sirius civilizations, you are not originally from there. You come from an older civilization that almost became extinct. We have learned to integrate and mingle with other civilizations. Your greatest lesson learned from each incarnation has been the nature of survival. Do you dare to find the beauty in the most base or lowly souls whose darkness overflows without any thoughts to walk into the light? You are learning to walk toward them fearlessly and to show them love to recover. Even the soul who has the most darkness can, by grace, find the light. Violent conquerers such as Napoleon, Alexander The Great, Hitler, Mussolini, Genghis Kahn, and others who came to the Earth devoid of a higher consciousness and did not value the human soul by killing and conquering innocent lives in a large scale. If you search to find these souls you will see that they have incarnated again to learn the lessons of being a better part of the human race. Remember, each and everyone of you has a connection to what you may refer to as extra-terrestrial origins. Much like an immigrant, some of you are delegates similar to representing these nations. You represent the Annunaki in this life time. You've had the experience of visiting many civilizations both terrestrial and extraterrestrial. Do you remember your trip one night when you slept where you had a lucid dream of walking with a number of people who looked very human and the environment was very similar to a business district. The place appeared as a white mall in a way. You were aware that none of them were human and they were aware that you were visiting their space. You were guided by a friend who protected you in this foreign place. You both walked down hallways, doorways and low stairs to get across the space. You were brought there to show the Annunaki who you were and what your purpose was. Both male and female gazed upon you but never to a point of feeling uncomfortable. In the end, you were given a quick kiss. Do you know who that was? He had been with you other life times before."

My mind raced as she described the dream. I remembered the dream clearly in my mind, but I don't remember seeing the face of my guide. His kiss was a quick peck on the lips, and it lacked any passion at the end of our tour of this place. " I remember the dream but I don't know who he is. I felt like I knew him somehow but he didn't seem right at the time. I mean, he seemed very serious and about his business. I can't recall who he was or where I met him."

I then shifted to a reading that I did where the same feeling came over me and I could see another all white space, similar to my dream. The man whom I was doing the reading was an ancient Sumerian in another lifetime. He was selected to be trained under the guidance of the Annunaki. It looked like the inside of a space craft without the driving mechanisms or control panels in view. Maybe it was more like a conference hall that was designated exclusively for training. Everything was white from floor to ceiling. There were slight curves in the architectural lines rather than corners or edges. Right through the center of the space was a long connected unit that had half moon shaped benches that would curve in like a scalloped effect housing multiple people in an even and orderly manner. Each bench had six people who were being trained. In front of them was a round table and a teacher or trainer in front of the table facing them. The discussions were always to the groups, never individuals. It seemed as if this craft was hovering above ground and not necessarily visible to the general population of Sumeria, and students were hand-picked or selected for a specific reason or purpose. Each student would retain the higher knowledge that would assist them throughout lifetimes. For example, the memory would return in Ancient Greece as philosophy and other mathematical sciences. Each age would awaken a portion of the knowledge at certain integrals of history as an old memory. When they were complete with their training they would step off the craft and forget the training and integrate into their society bringing higher knowledge of the sciences, biology and more to help in the evolution of mankind.

"A new star gate is opening up, as we speak, that is quite different from the ones in the past. This will allow you and many others to enter into a wisdom you once knew. It is within all of your power to save the Earth and to raise it in consciousness. You were never prepared to hear this information until now. It took you a while to raise in understanding since we first connected to you as a child. When you did climb and rise you had to encounter the dark shadows of Cruel Jack (Jack the Ripper) who had run rampage on the West (U.S.) and England in the past. We searched for him for a millennium and everyone suffered from his mighty blow. He had harmed many innocent children and people on the etheric realm...as you now know. This is the spirit behind all the cruelties against innocent children, that have to go. You have dealt with him on his Earthly incarnation and in time he will let go of all his hatred toward God's creation. Lift your eyes into the skies and ride upon the wings in flight for within the battle of other-dimensional fight you will be the victor of this evil in one night. This is your gift and your journey of light to help the people within your natural sight and float and fly to heavens abode and seek the wisdom we have showed. Then you will be able to arise with others in the skies."

Then I saw guardian beings wearing capes of blue and onyx made of wool and a bright metallic circular high collar that created a U shape behind their heads. Each guardian priest wears an amber stone...There are six priests or guardians there in an equal balance of three males and three females. The amber stone carries the mysteries of life from the inception of the planet. Each priest wears an amethyst ring on their right forefinger in the shape of a pyramid. This ring symbolized their connection to the Great Sky God or Sun God RA. There is an engraving resting in the fifth dimension, the all seeing eye of RA. This is a commitment of a never-ending resource of power of light that prevents our planet from any type of major destruction. A cycle hangs above those who challenge this power. These are the beings who were here to assist the great powers of Atlantis, Egypt and Mayan cultures that we know about today. The priests of this 5th dimensional space had at one time gone too far and tried to progress the humans in knowledge at a much faster rate before they had a full understanding and a higher consciousness. This is when the guardians stepped in and allowed others to conquer the Egyptians. The priests were returned to the Fifth Dimension and asked to assist with smaller doses of transmissions to continue on this process. They have had influences over many other great cultures such as Greece and early Rome, and our culture today throughout all civilized nations, to a lesser degree. They escorted the great thinkers of the Atlanteans through other cultures by way of the obscure Etruscan tribes. The Etruscan tribes had the higher knowledge that was dormant until their seed began to integrate and brought the rise of Greece and then Rome. Today, they still integrate your society with great memories of evolved beings who were capable of having such an advanced society as Atlantis. You were born into a lineage of the Etruscan seed in this lifetime.

Survivors of the Lemurian destruction were angered by the planet's decision to destroy their utopian society. The people did not realize that it needed to integrate and help the others around them. They were too focused on the core group as it brought great joy and gratification. They had a higher purpose of becoming more expansive by sharing their healing energy throughout the Earth and into darker regions of less evolved beings. Eventually, they would have expanded throughout the galaxy. We have been trying to send healing to them and teach them to help those who are less enlightened without reservation or withholding love from them.

The Atlantean Society went on to expand and reach out to other societies. When we allowed the darker beings to enter the portal, and they began to clone humans and other atrocities such as breeding animals with humans, this created a greater rift.This horror could have been avoided had they not turned away from them but rather assisted them in the process of integration. Because they were rejected as light beings, they rebelled and brought great nightmares to the human realm. Today, many of these beings have integrated and are working in our areas of science and innovation. Many of them have learned and grown beyond the Lemurians who are still stuck in a place of judgement. It is time for all to return to more simplistic ways of life. It is a time to seek the higher realms and pleasures of the Earth rather than escaping into non-realities and fantasies that can not be achieved in this natural realm. The pureness of food, water, earth should be restored. The love of family, friends and kindness to strangers should be returned. The fear of other humans will subside as the guardians are assisting the process of clearing the energy life forms who have been here to create illusion and destruction to humans. There is no need to worry; it will all be resolved on other dimensional realms. You will progressively feel lighter, happier, and clearer in your thinking. You will begin to feel harmony and the deepest love of the God Source. All of this has been blocked from people unless they made a strong effort to seek it out. In time, the Earth's energy will breath out love to all, even those who are in a much lower state of consciousness who desperately desire to raise up but don't know how.

On Atlantis, information was retrieved through crystal vibrations and a strong networking system of energy. The Atlanteans introduced much of the Lemurian knowledge and the knowledge of RA through a gateway. The

Crystal Skulls were created during this unrecorded time in our history to keep the information flowing throughout the masses. The information was on a crystal grid originally created by the Lemurian and then it evolved to a more finely tuned networking system that covered the planet. There were no longer pockets of land that were uninformed. This is what we realize to be as the Christ-consciousness grid. The same grid used to spread the news about Jesus Christ as he was sent from this dimensional realm to teach and assist the raising of consciousness.

Not all civilizations or uncivilized beings wanted to live on Atlantis. There were many other civilizations thriving at the same time, such as in South America and the Middle East, Asia and Africa. However, Atlantis was the highest mecca of power and strength that was unmatched by any other civilization before or after. We are not able to find this civilization in the natural realm because we must raise in consciousness for it to rise and become revealed. There are cultures that have thrived and disappeared in the past that we are not able to discover because there was a shift in the dimensional realms, much like the Anasazi, whose dwellings exist but the people had disappeared. Remnants of barrier walls and other artifacts lay dormant under the Atlantic ocean and have been mistaken for artifacts from other societies instead.

When the destruction occurred on Atlantis, the most important artifacts were retained and protected such as the Crystal Skulls.

The attributes of the Atlanteans were similar to the Lemurians in a way that they were able to transform their bodies."

My mind shifted again to a reading I had with a woman who sat directly across from me at my dining room table. I was just learning to read or provide insight to people and I was not prepared for what would happen. The woman looked like the average suburban house wife. She was kind and loved her family and friends and was surrounded by a happy environment. Being spiritual already, she was on her journey to understand who she was. We sat across from each other in fun anticipation. I closed my eyes and an other-worldly vision began to unfold. There was a priest, with fair skin, who stood before me in a red-metallic robe with a strand of white trim of material going down the middle, from the top to the bottom. He looked extraterrestrial and was wearing an unusual red hat. Then I saw a strange landscape of rocky terrain in red or russet earth. There were houses that were oval shaped or shaped as an egg. They were resting on high platforms or stands that were narrow and then got increasingly wider by the base for perfect balance of this structure. They also had a red metallic appearance. Then I saw a scene of a door sliding open horizontally and a similar priest emerged from one of the houses and I observed the stairs unfold out of nothing. From air they came down and unfolded into matter as a solid stairway leading down to the ground. He then descended, not by walking but revealing to me that his body was as malleable as liquid metal, melting down the stairs and then returning back to the form or structure as a being that I could recognize that looked similar to human form. I didn't know what this was. They refused to tell me who they were. It wasn't until I was at a Lemurian event that I saw artwork from a channeled artist who drew images of swirling geometric shapes. They displayed it on a wide screen for all of us to view and before my very eyes the city of these beings were revealed to me again. The artwork, though not in detail, displayed formations of the landscape that I had seen previously during this reading. It was the true Lemurians who had visited me through the reading and had guided me to many truths for the next few years. I finally understood why they were on such high, stilt-like structures. The were their watch towers when the planet filled with water. It was the planet Neptune. Some confuse Neptune, their king, with Poseidon. Although it may appear they are the same and historians tell us that the Greek and the Roman god were the same, with the exception of a changed name. This, however, was not true. Jupiter was not Zeus, some of the beings may have been the same but I am positive that some of them were entirely different and had a different purpose or contribution to our planet.

This was the space where I saw the black beings hovering over the water. This was the underwater scene of my earliest incarnations, within the dense water that I could seamlessly move through because of my etheric body. This kingdom was ruled by Neptune. When the darkness invaded that planet, Neptune became tainted and controlled by the darkest of beings in our galaxy. Many other Lemurians escaped and were escorted to Earth. The wisest ones went into the fifth dimensional space to supervise and assist. Neptune, carrying his trident or pitchfork, gathered the darker host and followed the rest to Earth. Now being fully under the control of darkness, he began to form an alliance of beings in the middle earth arising to power of unbelievable proportions. This was not Lucifer. Lucifer was a fallen angel from another realm, yet they did have an alliance that was significant from the beginning of human life on this planet. Neptune, was regarded loosely as the being we refer to as Satan. However, satanic power was not only one being but rather a collective of beings originating with the dark amphibians that invaded the Neptunian pure light. These Amphibian or Formorians, as referred to in Tom Cowan's book, *Fire in the Head, Shamanism and the Celtic Spirit. Mr. Cowan* mentions that they are located in the ocean and confirm the vision of how I saw them as amphibians and that they are huge, monstrous, misshapen beings who hold the space of darkness, night, and chaos. He refers to them as a cosmic evil. I would further say they have been used throughout realms to hold the space of contrast from light for the operations and expressions of free will and choice. In Christianity, these beings were referred to as demons. As in my vision, they were pure black and appeared as some type of whale-like bodies that when converged appear as a sheet of black. Either way, I felt a type of closure and surrender to my understanding and exploration of the paranormal. It was disturbing at times, yet, I felt a silent surrender always knowing that I was safe. The Earth has undergone many trials and yet, still exists. We've had many visitations, and yet, we still survive. When we remember our divine rights to our own bodies and the Earth, we will do even better. Regardless of what ever evil may come, we are protected and safe if we choose a higher place of consciousness and awakening. There will always be a balance and the light will always reign superior to any challenge that could arise.

Chapter Seventeen

Mysteries of The Sacred Red Stone

It was a beautiful fall evening with colored leaves of amber, yellow, and deep russet falling from the trees. There was nothing to compare to the autumn in New England. The rich colors made me reminiscent of hay rides, Halloween, pumpkin pie spice and Thanksgiving. This is the time when the veils are slightly lifted so we can see deeper into the other realms of existence. I was full of curiosity about all that was happening around me. And yet, I was beginning to settle into the seasonal change that meant snow drifts and colder weather were up ahead. I watched a beautiful sunset the night before. It appeared to be the artwork of the Earth that displayed a brilliantly lit, bold, orange-golden sunset. I wasn't particularly happy about the cold winter snows drifting in but the view could often be spectacular.

A friend contacted me and wanted to have a reading done. It was in the evening and after a long day at work, I welcomed her in and we shared a cup of tea while speaking about general topics related to her day. Our conversations were light and assisted in the process of helping her to relax. I would be the one doing the reading. However, it is much easier to do this if people feel comfortable and are prepared to hear their message. Being an empath, I found that I felt less stress in the process.

My friend has a very typical life today. There is nothing out of the ordinary that one would suspect that she had a much more powerful role in the past. I began the reading and was transported to England. The scene opened up to a strange spiritual place in Glastonbury. Before me stood a large stone that was carved out in the interior. The ceiling allowed the sunlight and constellations through a small circular window of seven or eight inches in diameter. From a logical standpoint, the window served the purpose of letting in minimal light to view the interior. However, it was revealed through my vision that the hole was an access of communication from the energy that was within. It was a form of a communication control room for extraterrestrial contact or the gods of these ancient people. I felt the Gladstone was called The Crypt of Knowing. It appeared to be highly spiritual, metaphysical, and sacred.

The interior of the crypt was magnificent. It was approximately seven to eight feet in diameter. There was a bed of quartz crystals that were clear and uncut that were strewn across the floor and a pure dense quartz crystal steps went directly from the front and to the back and parted around a large red stone that appeared to be a luminous ruby. Portions of the stone were removed and placed in various locations of the earth to assist the high priests in their ability to communicate and connect to the higher power. There, toward the back, was a carved shelf that held a sacred tablet that was similar to the Rosetta Stone. Two different languages were carved into the stone for instruction, guidance and prayer. On one side of the stone it was written in Phoenician and on the other side of the stone it was written in Egyptian. The Red Stone and process of using energy that was ignited by the sacred words had all come from Atlantis.

I looked and observed to see that it was my friend who was the male high priest there. He was wearing a long robe in white with a golden rope style belt that tied around the waist. He had silver grey hair cut bluntly to the shoulders, with bangs, and a medium length white beard. He wore a type of sandals and had a bell in his right hand. He was the caretaker of the Sacred Crypt. In another life she was also a scribe in Egypt. All of this began to come together.

I observed the Priest enter into the Crypt and the red stone began to glow. The crystals would rise up inches from the ground as if they were propelled by a magnetic floor. He then reached forward and lifted the stone tablet to read out loud the sacred mantra or words in Egyptian. Then he returned to the entryway as he observed a beam of light that was propelled from the red stone as a pillar of light that rose up from the gladstone window and permeated deep into the higher realms. The crystals began to rise up three feet higher as the floor became charged with energy and they swirled clockwise in a slow moving action around the beam of light that came from the red stone. Particles of light emitted from the crystals as they swirled around creating, what appeared to be, a fibre optic string of circular images and at time being a trail of particles again similar to a meteor's trail behind it.

In the past, this method would assist ancient Egyptian Priests to connect to RA and search out information that helped them find information and assist them with foresight of any danger or natural disasters. This sacred process was not abused or used to harm anyone or anything around them with the exception of protection against aggressors.

Because the Crypt as so sacred, rather than allow it to enter into the wrong hands, the Higher Beings allowed the tablets to be stolen by a local thief who carefully broke the tablet in two from the ceiling window and lifted each piece out, covered them in a blanket and was heading out to another town to sell it. Not knowing the mystical nature of the stone, the thief ignorantly thought he could handle the power it contained. He didn't travel more than ten feet when the tablet completely disintegrated as dust within the blanket and the energy from the central red stone released it's powerful light back up into the heavens. He also died from his exposure to violation of a sacred site. The crypt no longer worked the same way again and to the great dismay of my friend, the Priest, he was filled with tremendous guilt for allowing such a thing to happen. The entry way was never violated and continued to be hard to permeate. The door was made of a very hard wood and very thick with brass nails that were hammered deeply through the door. There was a lock and a long key that opened the door. The Priest wore the key around his neck at all times. The key was never taken from him and he was surprised that this happened. On typical occasions, the top of the crypt was too powerful for the average human to enter. He was full of self blame and loathing and died soon after, not fully understanding what had happened and unable to communicate with the higher beings again. My message to my friend was that they didn't hold her responsible for this event. It was the destiny of the Sacred Gladstone Crypt to be disassembled for the safety of human life. They knew that the Priest would be dying soon after and there was no one pure enough to entrust with this sacred communication as an apprentice.

As soon as the priest died many pagan and other locals entered the space and began taking objects from the crypt. It was difficult to take the Ruby stone from there so they would chip off large sections at a time and the stone traveled throughout the earth.

Two years had passed until I was asked to visit another woman's house who was having a small group of spiritual and highly respected guests over to learn more about what their soul connection was through a group Akashic reading. They were curious about what kept them together and what happened in the past.

The first lifetime was very significant and it involved all of them working together in an effort to remove a drought in Egypt. There were a few priests, a few priestess virgins and, a well respected family of Egypt. This ceremony did not involve the royal family as the people felt that they were disconnected from the citizens and only concerned about their family and personal agendas during the time when I high potential for famine was looming over them.

The houseguest of my visit was actually the matriarch of the family whose lineage was then traced back to ancient Egypt. They entered one of the temples and she opened up a mahogany box then lifted from it a beautiful woven cloth covered object. She then unfolded the beautifully woven silk cloth that revealed a red stone of power. This stone was sacred to the Ancient Atlanteans and was used for mystical and communicative purposes. She then inserted it into a specific place in the temple and soon after, the sky began to rain drops of healing water that began to replenish the Earth. The woman's generous gift of a family treasure made her a hero and beloved amongst the people. It was a while before Egypt would suffer from famine again. Many years later the stone would be taken by crusaders back to Rome.

The stone was then used for evil purposes and I believe that Merlin had also used this stone that was originally extracted from the Gladstone Crypt in Glastonbury, to gain power from the heavens and unleashed his own form of controls and darkness from hell.

I did another reading, many months after the group reading of the women and a few years after my friend. This woman was having personal challenges with her life and I suggested that she have an Akashic reading done. She was willing to face whatever came up so she could return to a happier state of being.

The scene opened up in an early settlement on the British Isles. I kept hearing the name Donegal and later discovered that there was a region in Ireland called Donegal. Yet, I was fully convinced that this was the link I was looking for and I shared this story with an Irish friend who thought the tale or reading matched something that he was familiar with, possibly a Scottish lineage from the MacDougall Clan.

There was a group of fierce men who traveled by horse from one village to another to pillage, rape and burn the villages for their mere pleasure. Their consciousness was from the depths of darkness and they had no remorse for their deeds of wickedness. The leader, appeared as an ancient Scythian from the steppes of Russia. His cloak was made of white rabbit pelts and other small animals. He was large, almost a giant, and his voice echoed in a way that immobilized his prey as a lions roar would frighten an animal before they could run. Then I saw it. He was wearing a ring in brilliant red fiery light that was surrounded by ornate metal scrolling designs. I knew this ring gave him power and believe it came from the Gladstone.

The scene shifted and I observed a woman (The woman who was receiving the reading), as she walked by her cottage gathering eggs from chickens and picking things from her garden, when I heard, "She is a Common woman." I understood that she was poor but couldn't quite figure out why they made a point to say it that way. I discovered later, when I researched a bit that the Mac Dougall's were kinsmen of the Comyns.

As I observed the woman by her garden, I could see the group of men riding up from the east of the cottage. There were two men from the village who were designated as gatekeepers or protectors of their people. One was a valiant warrior who fought many battles and whose personality was quite humble. The other, was a boisterous fellow whose bark was bigger than his bite at times. The two of them stood watch as the intruders came fiercely over the rolling hills of green. The leader had a power around him and the the gatekeepers had a formidable dread of seeing his white pelt cloak flying in the wind as he approached.

The air was still and the two men gathered their courage, but to no avail. He approached them and spoke with a deep guttural sound. Then glanced toward the cottage and watched the woman near her home, alone and awaiting her husband to return. No one said a word to dissuade him from approaching the woman who was as frail and vulnerable as the rabbit pelts he strewn across his broad shoulders. The woman was raped and murdered on the site and then he road off knowing that her husband would come find him. He set back awaiting a later battle.

Time elapsed when the husband returned to discover that his wife had been taken from him. He never pursued the group of men for fear that others would become vulnerable, and he decided to keep watch over the village for the remainder of his life. I became his mistress in time and we could never be together because of this fury and never ending warfare in that region.

While reading the legend, I discovered later that Robert the Bruce, had the Celtic Brooch of Lorne that he wore, and it was a family heirloom. The MacDougall Clan at one time took that Brooch from him. When I observed the picture of the Brooch, the design, not the stone color, was identical to my vision of the ring that the leader wore during his height of his tirade against the vulnerable local villages.

I had two other readings after this that added more information to the story. I saw a small village, as mentioned previously, about a group of people who were being harassed by small groups of men from various villages to pillage, rape and burn down neighboring clans. This was to get access to food sources and keep the competition weak or overtake more land. The incident in this case arises from a woman who clung to a knight for protection and ultimately, King Arthur rises up to become the protector.

This incident preceded the events mentioned regarding the MacDougalls, but was typical behavior for many generations in this part of the world.

Another reading revealed an ancient curse that was sent to a Scottish family who were also alive during the time of the MacDougalls. Could the origin of all of this be equated with the misuse of an ancient stone? Anything is possible. Here is an opportunity to consider the gift of knowledge or wisdom would be handed more freely to humankind if they would have a sense of consciousness of using the power of knowledge exclusively for the good.

Getting back to the Wayside Inn, in Sudbury MA, the name of the school was called The Redstone Schoolhouse...This is another piece of information to ponder.

Chapter Eighteen

Atlantis Rising With The Sun

A new window began to open up as visions of Atlantis began to flow like a seamless unending dream. I had a vision of the survivors of Lemuria, including myself, emerging from Stonehenge where we opened the gateway to build a new city. In more recent times, the confirmation of this power could be revealed through an enormous amount of crop circles with messages from outer space, other dimensions and higher beings who want to usher in a higher consciousness.

Atlantis became what one would refer to as a city of light. They traveled across the continents easily lifting themselves in a molecular space transportation and then arrived at the ocean edge of the Atlantic. The tectonic plates under the ocean began to move as the land mass was called forth to form a volcanic wave. The Earth lifted high into the sky then gently molded into habitable land. The mountainous spread made way for large buildings made of crystals. Crystal pyramids were laid throughout the Earth to hold the waters of the firmament in place. These were the waters above the Earth that created a shield from the harmful ultraviolet rays and kept moisture in the Earth for all inhabitants. When they came to this land they began to build large buildings in four directions. The primary buildings were very tall and made of crystal that was shaped as a pyramid with a flat faced surface. The crystal had a greenish/blue hue to it from reflections of the sky and water. This created an emerald green city overlooking the azure blue ocean. It was breathtaking to behold. Other living spaces and smaller quarters were delightful to view.

They created their cities in ways unknown to our current technology. There were palm trees and orange groves, pineapple, lemon and limes in abundance. There were other fruit trees and vegetables that were also in abundance, some of which are now extinct such as a raised, bumpy orange-skinned fruit with a white, creamy center and blue seed. This fruit was one of the staples of the Atlantean diet, and it helped them stay healthy and full of vitality. Some believed that it contributed to their longevity. The Atlanteans were vegetarians, slim with dark hair and tanned skin. There were some blondes. However, the vision I saw was a time when they all appeared like this. I know that in both cultures, the Lemurians and Atlanteans had dark hair. I have also read the possibility that there were a lot of redheaded Atlanteans as well.

Getting back to my vision, the hair color would distinguish the young from the old. The wonderful ageless faces with snow white hair revealed the wisdom of an elder and the garment of a specific color told more. Intuition was extremely high and being telepathic and highly attuned to one another created an environment of honesty, integrity and minimal criminal behavior, if any at all. Each person experienced a level of abundance in all aspects of their lives being able to work with not only the laws of attraction, but also the laws of creation that were available to them before the civilization fell. They lived in a utopian society if compared to how we live today. The landscape was breathtaking with vines of fragrant flowers and manicured ornamental plants. Each person had the ability to create their own space or atmosphere through their thoughts or the power of the mind. I didn't notice anyone doing physical labor. Everything or anything that one could imagine was being created.

It may appear to be perfect in many ways. However, there were problems there as there are in any society. This is how it was in the beginning. Toward the middle and the end it was not so as others integrated their society.

There were majestic crystals, amber stones and amethyst rings found. In the vision, the rings had power and ended up in various locations of the earth. Some of them had a sacred red stone in them. There are other stories that came up that interwove tales of these red stones that came up in various readings from many different people who were not connected to one another as the stories would unfold during a much later time in history.

The destruction of Atlantis has been explained in many ways. For some, there are not enough archaeological remnants left behind to validate this complex and advanced societal existence. Some theorize that the high powered energy of the Bermuda Triangle came from energy sources that were once Atlantean crystals or objects with properties related to anti-matter, similar to the Philadelphia Experiment. This could potentially explain the change of solid matter into particles that transported and regrouped at another location. It could also be an entrance process into other dimensional worlds similar to the story *Prescott's Waiting* as I shared earlier in another chapter. Another idea could open up to the extraterrestrial realms of the unexplained existence of portals, doorways, or windows that open up to time/space realities. I once did a reading for a client whose past life opened up into Egypt where I was with her performing a ceremony, surrounded by the pyramids and many others. The scene created a blur or have some abnormal waves and then the landscape changed as we were all transported to a Mayan temple in South America. The step pyramid was clearly not the same as the Egyptian pyramids we had previously seen. The tropical rainforest was strikingly South American. I have no idea how this happened as I observed it in the Akashic records I knew it happened and was recorded. However, the process or objects used to create this unusual group transport was not revealed to me or available for my access when I asked about how it all happened.

Others believe that everything in Atlantis was etheric, not solid matter, and could only be seen through a dimensional lens of the third eye. For here is the place that unveils universal truths of reality beyond veils of solid matter. If both Lemuria and Atlantis were etheric locations on our

Earth plane, so would be Avalon, El Dorado, Shangri La, and others. It is possible that many of these existences were in a reality in our ancient history including tales of the Norse, Greek, Romans and Biblical references of Longevity, Roman and Greek Gods (who were most likely the Annunaki), and the Norse Aryan beings.

Here is an explanation of what I saw, whether or not it was real is something to be debated. I observe, see and record the likeness of images without the scientific knowledge to interpret the minute details related to any natural or supernatural event.

The scene of my vision unfolded as I was observing the continent of Atlantis prepared to view the last moments that lead up to its destruction. I witnessed two types of phenomenon occurring at the same time. The first was an enormous energy wave, beacon or pillar of energy rising up from the core of the Earth. This wave moved up through the center of the continent and then surrounded the continent out and around in a spherical motion of energy that covered the entire continent like a snow globe. This had a wave-like energy if observed from another plateau or beyond the continent whether one was on land or sea. It had a misty hue to it at times. This is where I saw a strong similarity between it and the legend of Avalon, an emerald green terrarium of a misty sunlit utopia. This was a strong magnetic energy field that served the purpose of protection and environmental balance, because of some of the effects of a previous fall and the earth access tilt that kept the environment out of balance. Within this system a consistent natural environment had been restored as the earth was originally intended. Still, the firmament had not collapsed and the water shelf up above remained. Other factors seemed to come to play in which Atlanteans needed to fabricate this environment as they were previously accustomed to this.

The second phenomena was beneath the snow globe of energy and even deeper below the continent. There appeared a smoldering mountain of molten volcanic lava. I observed the explosion of a volcanic eruption beneath the water as it rose up to collide with the magnetic energy sphere around the surface. The etheric objects surrounded the continent like an electrical fire or fire ball that neutralized the magnetic field. Having a deeper connection to their surroundings, the people of Atlantis jumped into boats and began to exit the land desperate to survive. Some had already left as I observed the King of Atlantis sitting on another continent watching the entire continent sink. As the continent began to sink it was an ocean full of people trying to swim to shelter, similar to Lemuria. Many did not make it. Those who did ended up in South America. This is where I ended up for the duration of my life during that time.

My vision then changed to images of what the city looked like before the destruction. For some unexplained reason, my memory began with the destruction and then they showed me more details about the city.

A city of immeasurable beauty opened up to me as I observed these tall white columns or pillars set perfectly in the north, south , east and west of the city. On top of each pillar was a crystal skull communication device. The energy flowed in a very fibre optic method. The skull would light up and glow to transmit and receive information. Other skulls were set on the borders of neighboring continents and around the Earth. This is how they kept in communication with what was happening, similar to the functions of our satellites. However, this was much less invasive to our environment and much less costly and efficient as networks of communication. These skulls were given from the fifth dimensional plane of RA, the Sun God or People of the Sun. They not only had communication with the rest of the earth but also communication with RA and the guardians who existed there. Though the other cities and dwellings around the Earth also had access to this information, they were significantly less advanced, organized and lacked power.

After the destruction, many of the powerful leaders of Atlantis chose to rise up to stay in the fifth dimension with RA. Others chose to stay, such as myself, to continue to assist with the evolution of the planet. Similar to Egypt, the knowledge and intervention of higher beings were preventing the pure evolution of the human race because they were taking in the advancements without the purity of heart that showed an acceptance of others on the planet who were different and had various levels of consciousness, racial differences and gender differences, etc.

During a meditation I encountered a being who escorted me to a crystal water path. He was very tall and wore a long robe. The path seemed to glisten with diamonds. He brought me up to a gate and then told me to turn around. I looked and observed a beautiful landscape of trees and green earth. It was the night and I could see the stars in the sky. Then I heard the words, "You are not ready yet." I returned from my vision, finding myself seated comfortably on my living room couch.

Not content with the vision, I returned into meditation again and there was a scene of a native man who needed help. I was also native but he was not of our tribe. He asked me to escort him across a lake with my canoe. When he got on his canoe I noticed that his skin was perfect, almost flawless and his clothing was very clean. He gazed deeply into my eyes as if I should know him. It felt uncomfortable and I began to ask questions who he was. He told me his name was Flow Tide. I thought it was unusual to have two names describing the motion of water. Being native, that concept wasn't altogether strange but still, I could see he was from another origin not anywhere near us at the time. We had an affair and he stayed with my tribe and then departed, saying he would see me another time in the future. I then saw him by the water's edge observing the destruction of Atlantis. It was the King of Atlantis who safely traveled to the waters edge before the destruction. He did not flee from his people. He was protected because of his wisdom and the role that he was to play in the future. The scene then changed again and there I was at the gate entering into the gate this time being escorted by Flow Tide. There were many people there awaiting my visit as they greeted me and remembered me from Atlantis.

They said,"Atlantis is rising again." We mustn't haste our efforts to raise back into this consciousness. You, as well as many others, will begin to remember the wonderful quality of life we once had. We live this way now in the 5th dimension. You can live this way on Earth if you choose." I knew what he was saying and then my eyes opened to my reality of life, my home, my couch, my living room. I stood up and walked over to the door and stepped outside. My surroundings were filled with green grass, shrubs and arborvitaes carefully planted to border the street. The sounds of birds sang with delight and I sat peacefully on my front stairs. The noise of the traffic became muffled as my eyes drifted back to my previous visions of Atlantis. I wanted to remember again. All this was recorded on a notebook when it happened so I would never forget its beauty. I could now, for the first time, begin to see the beauty of Atlantis had never left. It still remained in my natural surroundings. The Earth was still breathing the magnificence of perfection. The very essence of life incapsulated with all that appealed to the human senses and all that stirred our curiosity. The small creatures of bugs, plants, water droplets, birds, snakes, cats, dogs, skunks, rabbits, and the friendly groundhogs that created burrowing holes in my back yard. The funny faces of animals challenging me to enter their domain and the swooping bird of mischievous taunting fervor, made me laugh. I brushed past a butterfly bush where very large bumble bees circled around my head and a hornet's nest tucked up under the roof's edge. I giggled to myself as I entered my house again to clean and get the laundry done. My guinea pigs Crumbcake and Bucky dashed within their cage and called out in silly sounds of communication demanding their daily hay and fresh vegetables.

I reached into the refrigerator to gather some carrots and celery when I began to giggle about the silliness around me. I felt truly happy. I felt very connected to the Earth in a way that I had never noticed before. If none of these visions mattered and I finally found inner peace and connectedness to the Earth, then all of this was worth it... I gazed outside the window after feeding my guinea pigs and there was the groundhog, right up close to the house, glaring at me with squinted eyes in a territorial challenge. The thought of me actually being the owner of the property was not something he was willing to accept. I laughed again and in my own way communicated with him that he was right and I would not ever do anything to make him leave. I thought about the skunk that I ran into a few evenings earlier who I thought was a cat when it brushed past my legs without spraying me. Don't ask me how that happened, but I equally found them quite amusing.

Many of the Atlanteans are here with us today. They incarnated and had contributed their wonderful gifts of life, knowledge and higher consciousness around us. Many are spiritual leaders or teachers. Most of them do energy healing work and many are humanitarian and have a strong desire to help animals and in particular, water mammals because they know the importance of the dolphins and whales who help our planet keep balanced. They also have a similar form of communication to the crystal sculls that help keeps the oceans in perfect health. The interference of sound waves and tones could be highly detrimental to all living things. We must abandon unnatural tones underwater as it could launch unsuspected natural disasters. We should see the dolphins and whales as sacred beings who are here to help us raise in our consciousness of existence that allows the human race to continue to thrive.

Months had passed and I was unsuspectedly awakened by a dream. I knew that the feeling of Atlantis had returned to me and more was coming through. I could see the most breathtaking view of a building in white that almost looked like a wedding cake. Their were tiers of ornate banisters of carved angels and floral reliefs. The building was pure white, circular and very tall. There were people in white robes similar to a romanesque painting of the angels or gods as they looked out into the city with love and adoring eyes. Then I saw myself, with pure white hair but I looked very youthful in my face. Maybe mid to late 20s in age. My hair style was similar to an earlier vision where I had bangs and short, bluntly cut hair to the shoulders.

I was a priestess and with many other Priests and Priestesses, we stood in pairs, one facing toward the city and one facing toward the ocean. Each pair was set on one of the four corners of the city. There were both male and female. We stood on top of these very high buildings that appeared similar to step pyramids with a flat, shiny face of golden glass or crystalline material. Maybe it was some time of element or metal; I couldn't tell from my perspective because it was breathtaking as I stood on top of this building with the most magnificent view while reaching out to the sun lit sky of warmth and invigorating sunshine. The clouds were beautifully arranged to display a celestial glow and patterns of light that only the angels remember.

I was a mover of energy and could clear the energy from particles that could be detrimental to the well-being of the others. Some of it kept our air quality clear from natural pollutions and bacterias from falling cosmic debris. This daily effort and the role of all the priests and priestesses was to create positive energy flow with crystals that connected to the pre-planted crystal grid by the Lemurians. The Lemurians were there along with us to help us connect and activate these grids. Many stayed with us as guardians and advisors. We also introduced other stones and metals to enhance the original knowledge of the Lemurians. Other star people visited Atlantis and assisted our growth while introducing knowledge they had to enhance our purpose.

The problem we had later was a time period when the Atlanteans forgot their original purpose and began to become class minded and developed a form of racism from star beings who were different. These beings began to cause a rebellion because they knew that the Earth was intended for all extraterrestrials to amalgamate and assimilate to some degree. We were asked to learn from one another and to not be judgmental if a new society entered who had a lower consciousness than ours. They began to hold lesser value over plants and animals as we do today. Because of this blatant judgement against these beings they retaliated and began to use their scientific knowledge to create clones and mixing the genetics of animals and Atlanteans (humans) together and created beasts of horrifying appearances out of rebellion. Their statement was how they saw the monster within us through hatred and prejudice. The beasts were then recorded to be seen in later history as Satyrs, minotaurs and other half animal half human beings throughout the Greek and Roman histories, legends and myths. They were formidable creatures who caused problems and were carriers of hatred, anger, rebellion, disarray and as a form of judgement of mankind's prejudice. Today, these beings still exist on the astral plane or other dimensions as a pan-like being, or other gruesome horned and hooved creatures. Scientists and other researchers fully intrenched with the idea of cloning and cross-breeding were very likely the same beings who entered our atmosphere and had incarnated to remember the experiments they once performed out of a displaced feeling of rejection to the rest of the earth. I hope we can be finally healed and discontinue this rampage of vengeance in a natural Earth that has suffered too much already.

Returning once again to the city I notice a beautiful skyline of purple that casts hints of silver. Since this was the time of the pre-flood the atmosphere still had the firmament that reflected in silver. I thought about the saying, 'how the clouds had a silver lining.' The elements in the air would drop on occasion leaving a dewy moisture on the plants and the metal element would be preserved for and saved for rituals. We would also sprinkle light portions of it on our food to assist with longevity. I thought of the Hebrew manna that was given to the Jews during the forty years of wandering the wilderness. They seemed to survive off of this element. At certain times you could see a dusting of silver particles amongst the mist. We saw this as a blessing from the Gods. On a rare occasion the suns rays would sparkle with this silver mist and we would fall to our knees in adoration, because of its magnificent beauty, to our God or the Source of All Things.

I fell in love under the moon of Pluto which we could see. This is where the Priest was from. He was tall and serious, not one to play or fool around. He was the complete opposite of my whimsical, fairy-like, nature. The people of Atlantis saw my magic and asked me to watch over them and become their priestess for this very reason.

He came to our land and to our temple to assist in the dispersion of energy of another kind. He had rare gifts of time-travel and brilliance. He was soft-spoken, but stern, most people chose to not interact with him much but they all felt a deep respect for his wisdom and higher knowledge. He arrived after I had been stationed at this temple. Prior to that time, another priest was stationed next to me and he had a very pure soul. However, the people didn't feel that he had enough power to keep us safe. Then arrived the priest from Pluto. He called himself Shimeya. He was tall, muscular and tan with piercing blue eyes and brown hair that came to his shoulders. He stood out because no one else looked like him. Most of the inhabitants had black hair or very dark brown, blue, green, hazel (yellow hue) or brown eyes. The older people, like myself, had white hair.

The first time I worked with Shimeya I noticed an instant attraction between the two of us. It didn't feel like co-workers as when I worked with the other priest. I would feel his stare coming strongly through my skin from behind me. When I turned around it was a feeling of being captivated by his eyes. It wasn't necessarily the color but the depth of the stare that took my breath away. The sun shone brightly upon his hair as the lights reflected off him in a glow of pure glistening light. Embarrassed, I would fumble over myself trying to return to the daily responsibilities of my priestess duties. The first day we continued on like this and he began to speak with me as he noticed I was feeling uncomfortable and felt the attraction too overwhelming. When he began to speak with me I began to see visions of other planets and places that flashed before my eyes. Then I saw him...he was standing in front of me dressed in a blue wrap that covered only his waist down past his knees. He wore sandals and a necklace with shark's teeth or something like that. I appeared to be part amphibian or mermaid-like with legs. There were scales about my neck and back. He stared at me the same way. I was mesmerized by the vision and a strange feeling of knowingness came over me. I remember him now in some strange way at some distant time and place that I couldn't quite put my finger on. It was him, a love, a romance,...no it was more than that. It was a type of experience that one travels great distances and eclipses all time and space to discover once again.

The visions stopped and I looked over to him as he was standing to my left almost six feet or more away from me. His eyes were less intense, he brought me to a place of hypnosis where I could remember my past. At the same time, he could verify that I was the same life form or soul who he once remembered. Now his expression was much softer and extremely gentle. Apparently, there have been many other deceivers who have crossed his path portraying to be me. Not knowing who or what he was, I never thought to be anything else other than myself. With a very confused expression, I looked at him and said, "I know you from another time. There was another place where you and I were lovers, but I looked very strange and part amphibian."

At that point I finally realized he was highly attracted to me and I began feeling an overwhelming sense of love. I asked him, " Did we know each other in another past life?" He replied, "Yes, we were meant to be soul mates. I had chosen you for myself." He went on to say that I was created for him to be his wife or partner so he would feel a sense of balance and comfort. He told me that he searched 800 years for me. The darkness had covered me and changed my appearance. He had searched for me in oceans and other planets or realms of existence where I could have possibly landed through incarnation.

I asked him," How did you know it was me? He said, "Your eyes reveal your history, your many lives. I could see myself in your eyes. I want you to get to know me again. Our love was very rare and deep. It nearly destroyed me when you were lost. No one could fill my soul as you have."

The wind began to blow and a strange light fell upon us. He looked around and said, "They watch us, but there is nothing they can do. We are now together again. He blew me a kiss and all my fears subsided. I had an overwhelming urge to go swimming as my mind began to recall the feeling of fresh water touching my flesh. I was beginning to awaken to who I once was and the memories began flooding in. This lifetime as an amphibian was the last lifetime that I remembered who I was as a soul. It had been over 800 years since then. The dream like vision began to fade and there he stood before me with a gentle smile wearing an Etruscan robe that rested over one shoulder. His chest was strong with muscles and toned. His hair was hanging down to his shoulders with slight waves of golden brown and a head band of blue material, similar to the wrap he wore in my vision, held his hair from falling into his face. I watched him lift heavy pitchers of metallic powder or metallurgic elements and toss the dust into the atmosphere as it cleared the space with phenomenal force and perfection. The priests and priestesses across from me shook their heads and were confused that the work is done with one effort. Amazed, I turned around to see him and he glanced at me with kindness. He never used magic as we did. His method was much more efficient. I was humbled to see him work. I was even more enamored by his love and emotion toward me. It seemed simple, sincere and even had a feeling of purity. Beneath it all was a much deeper passion that was incredibly intense.

As soon as the clearing was done I was asked to perform a ceremony of thanks and gratitude to the gods. As I began to pray and deliver the offerings, a hand reached through a cloud and handed me a golden bowl. Shimeya watched me while I did my work and began to move my arms and hands in a way of moving the energy, that turned into a dance. After the ceremony was over, he mentioned that he was surprised to see the man make such great efforts to hand me the bowl and went on to say who he was in the higher realms. I felt that Shimeya was pleased to see that my heart was in the right place when he returned.

Shimeya asked me to spend some time together with him that was similar to the space he lived in when I met him. It was a cave that had grey reflective sparkling particles inlaid into it. It was not white stone like the typical Atlantean home. I immediately headed toward the walls to feel the texture of this cave. It all felt strikingly familiar as I gazed around the space, wide-eyed and curious as a child entering a hidden passage way where no one else could find them. He was amused by my curiosity and I found him smiling at me in an endearing way. He knew I was trying to figure out the alloys and other compositions employed in constructing this space as I was one of the builders of Atlantis. The cave seemed to match his strong, masculine exterior as he had an earthy connection as a wild hunter or warrior. My eyes now shifted to a golden bowl in the center of the room that held a beautiful blue flame of fire.

Shimeya asked me to sit across from him on a black fur rug from an animal skin. Underneath the rug were other rugs of texture and colors like tigers, leopards, zebra's, white bear skins and giraffe. It was a jungle room and many of the skins I had never seen before. We sat across from each other on these plush skins that were amazingly comfortable. I crossed my legs in the lotus position and so did he as we gazed into each other's eyes. I had a flash back of us in a prehistoric time with some of these animals roaming around us in the wild. It was the same stare, the entrance of a cave, and passionate love, too passionate for me to understand. I thought about our uneasiness of some other beings, not like us, observing our every move and behavior like lab mice. I was upset to see that we had revealed our intimacy to these beings during a very innocent time of human life and they came in to corrupt what we had and distort the Earth's reality. But who were these beings? My mind began to scan this reality because I knew them and have dealt with them, even in this life time.

He watched as my eyes began to flicker as if I went into a slight trance. He questioned, "What's wrong? Are you not feeling well?" I pulled myself from the vision and told him what I had just seen.

"You're beginning to remember." he said, in a slightly sad voice because of the nightmare of all that we had been through. "I never forgot. I kept my memory of every incident that ever happened. This has kept me safe but I've had some very dangerous situations and some very heartbreaking experiences that plummeted me deep into a very dark place of anger. I asked the Origins to protect you by sending you into the Karmic web to hide you and protect you from the horrible memories of our past. Now that you are remembering, this will be very difficult for you to deal with because of our innocence and their cruelty. It will be hard for you to forgive and get past it all. I know I had the challenge for many years. They destroyed something beautiful in us and wanted me to suffer forever. They knew I had power but didn't want me to have happiness as well. There were other women, but you were my perfect fit, my soul's choice. It is my fault that you have suffered the pains of these events. Today, you are still suffering for it. If they discover that I am here you will be in danger again."

"Who are these beings and why do they want to hurt us?"

"I can't explain that to you now but they want to control this planet and many others." They are searching for gold and other energy sources that are not attainable in other areas. They feed off of the energy of life and pull from humanity. I fight to keep the Earth protected as do others. They are an unseen force, yet manifest when they need to interact. You know who they are, they come to you in your dreams. It will be fine. I will have to leave and figure out how to take you with me. Will you come with me to another land where you will be safe?"

I looked at him in apprehension. After all, the feeling of being swept away by his charm and sensitivity was so alluring. I paused while thinking of the love we had in my vision. I could still feel it just being in his presence and his energy was magnetic and powerful as I felt myself slipping away in a fainting spell. In one moment, he was embracing me and held me tightly in his arms. My heart was racing but my body felt weak. He had some type of power over me and I didn't want to resist it. We spent long hours together that seemed to eclipse both time and space. There were long moments of communication that was purely telepathic and visions of light, explosions of creation, shifts of realities all converged into one as I basked in this euphoric ecstasy.

I know that I had received a download of information from him during that time. He brushed my hair from my face as we lay peacefully in each others arms on the animal skins. The hardest part to face was his rejection of me. He had longed to see me again and could have helped me much sooner but I had left him of my own free will.

I could see the pain in his eyes as if it just happened recently. I asked him to explain so I could understand what I did to cause him such pain.

He looked at me with hurt eyes and said, "You left me and went with them."

"I went with who? The people who were watching us in my vision when we were amongst the wild animals and rough terrain?"

"Yes, it was them."

"Please tell me how all of this happened. I can't see anything right now." I said with a concerned voice. There was an strong feeling of anxiety as I began to search deeper into his eyes for answers.

His eyes were downcast and then he looked away. He stood up and put his right hand on his head and searched for a way to explain what happened. He looked around the room scanning for something unseen to my eyes and then nodded his head as if having an internal conversation with himself or someone else. I waited patiently and watched him breathing heavy and carrying the pain from thousands of years of sorrow. I realized quickly that I could wait to hear when he was ready, since he had carried this pain for so long and I simply forgot after many incarnations of life times. I was the endless dates with a girlfriend who had amnesia and he had to keep reminding me who I was and what we had. I felt sick within my stomach and my mind. I felt troubled by the complexity of something so full of feeling yet so foreign and unknown.

"What could I have possibly done to cause such great pain?" I muttered softly as if in a train of thought that shouldn't have been spoken out loudly.

Overhearing me, he turned to me abruptly and said, "You made me fall in love with you. Just when I thought I could live without you, I would see you again and my heart would fall captive to your whims. I have great power and have achieved great things unknown to man. I have conquered many unconquerable men and captured the hearts of many beautiful woman. None could make me feel as you make me feel."

"You, in your simple mind of silliness, your innocence of Earth, and your curiosity like a child. It is you who has prevented me from finding joy without you. When they made you for me, I didn't believe that it would have such a strong affect upon my soul. I thought I could be gone without you. I thought I could discover something greater and better than what you held. I thought you would only be a faint memory. Instead, it has been a living nightmare to protect you, always concerned that the worst would happen and you would be eliminated all together. The gift I received from the Origin is the same gift I spurned. They asked me to help them in exchange for great pleasure and deep happiness. I thought they were tricking me into an illusion of false happiness. They called upon me into the depths of the Earth. They sent shooting stars along my path. They sent warriors of tremendous power in battle against me to challenge my strength. I accepted all challenges.

"The beings that observed us are from another race of beings. They are logical, rational and lack emotion in every area. They have the ability to run the planet efficiently but will never be able to understand humans and how they behave. They place harsh rules and standards that are not attainable which causes many to give up and retreat to addictions and other means of escape. The cruelties of life for humans are unnecessary. They were originally created in our likeness. We understand them."

"Who are your people?"

"We are the Annunaki. You are one of us. They kidnapped you and manipulated much of what has happened because of many incidences like this. They are beings we had helped in the past. Some of them were our slaves who had joined a coalition of these beings. They have been hard on you because you are here to help me."

"Many, many years ago, when I discovered you near the water, we fell in love. We spent time together and I began to teach you our ways. You were happy but had the attention span of a youthful child. You were whimsical being that liked to interact with many others. I realize that you had a greater purpose in your social personality, but I kept you isolated from everyone else. They knew the nature of being that you were and enticed you to go with them while leaving me behind."

We were talking by a grove of trees. laughing and enjoying our time together, when a portal opened. It was so beautiful and serene that day. The birds were chirping and the sun was at midday. I remember feeling lazy and wanting to rest while you entertained me with a story. We were laughing and enjoying each other's company when the door opened up into the other dimensions. They had laughter and sounds of celebrations with many people in a festive gathering. They enticed you to come. Being spontaneous and full of life you innocently ran over to see what was going on. I cried out to you realizing that it was a trap and yelled out to not enter the portal. It was too late. As soon as you entered the portal, the window closed behind you. I couldn't find you after that. Tormented by what happened, I thought you wanted to leave me."

While he spoke gently in tone and baring his soul about his pain, I began to remember the horrifying events that took place in another life time. I remember playfully dancing around while he sat watching me by a grove of trees. He was much more relaxed and had calming energy. I was much more energetic, much like a butterfly or bee jumping from one flower to the next. He was amused by my gestures and expressions and I was comforted by his peaceful and calming personality. He gave me comfort and love that far surpassed anything since. His wisdom was beyond my comprehension and so, to some degree, we didn't have a lot of depth in our conversation. In this sense he was beyond me. Although, it didn't matter to him, he loved me all the same. I remember the sounds of celebration and the enticement of that atmosphere. Without realizing what I was doing, I entered and crossed through the portal to soon discover that the party or festivity was only a facade. The door was now gone and I became imprisoned by these cruel beings who kept moving me from place to place. The rest became a blur. I looked at him in deep distress and sorrow.

"I remember it now. It was them, the beings who were watching us while we were together in the jungle. They were also the same ones who enticed me into their portal."

He let out a deep sigh and then said, "Yes, they are masters of deception." They want control and dominance over everything and they have manipulated many circumstances around me."

"What do they want from us or from you?"

"They want me to quit, to give up everything, to forfeit all I worked for and to allow them to dominate the Universe. They are a collective of beings who want control."

"What do you want? Were you controlling the Earth in the same way?"

"No, the Annunaki were guiding the Earth to evolve but they kept experiencing interferences and intervention that constantly disrupted the natural transition of all things. These other Beings don't want humans to raise up in consciousness to know who they are and that we, as their parent guardians love and care for them. These beings will eventually lead mankind to self-destruction and wars so they can repopulate the earth with like-minded beings. I can't allow that to happen. Our love is too great for this to happen."

His eyes were cast down in sorrow and then he looked up as if he was seeing someone in the heavens. I knew that my folly had been too much for him. Yet, he seemed to be independent of any anger toward me as he realized that I was too naive to understand what had happened. He never forewarned me of the potential trouble of their menacing behavior. Even he was caught off guard by their wily plan.

He reached out for my hand and then he pulled me in to his arms. It was all over. The discussion that we had forced us to come to a realization of a greater misunderstanding. A deeper call to service was now pulling him back, and he told me that something was going to happen to Atlantis and that I would end up in a safe place. He was not caught in our karmic wheel and would head off to other lands and obligations of his journey. I would survive but continue to feel the challenges of karma in lifetimes to come. Yet, the memory of him would be forever imprinted on my mind as I sit here today remembering him as if it was only a few years back that we had this encounter.

Our encounter and reuniting was significant mostly to us. The bigger picture that affected many others was corruption that had leaked into and permeated the consciousness of the Atlanteans. A perversion of humankind was set into place as they began the cross breeding of humans with animals and experimenting with the human genome for other purposes that were a violation to the human race. The Origin of All Things joined in agreement to stop the spread of these corruptions and plummeted the whole society into the sea. The great explosion from the volcano and magnetic shield annihilated this tropical paradise of futuristic magnificence. Some of the souls ascended into the 5th dimension. Many of the souls died and began their summit into the karmic wheel of life experiences. The third group survived who were not fully corrupted, nor were they truly evolved. They were the ones who made their way to America's. Some went to South America as the early Mayans, Incas and Aztec's. Some went to the North America as native tribes. Some went to Greece and mediterranean cultures as the Egyptians, Etruscans and ancient Greek cultures, Crete, Troy, and Persia. Some spread out further east to Japan. All of these displace people brought with them knowledge of higher education, organized governments, and forms of technology or advanced calendars, astronomy, biology, mathematics, science, and more.

I stepped into a brief window of viewing as I observed the offspring of the animal human beasts that they created. They were highly rebellious, disturbing to look at and they had a reaction to how they felt as monsters. They seemed to be devoid of a soul and reviled authority. They were so lawless that they caused great turmoil around the people while introducing new fears and nightmares that the people had never encountered before. These were the demons of fears and their spirits lasted for many years above the ethers of the planet, tormenting the innocent and their children. We have not been fully freed from these beasts who can not deliver themselves from this long-lasting hell. They never asked to be here or to be mistreated for how they were made. It was the works of others and experiments that should not have been done and a lesson to us now for allowing this on the Earth. Many still long for scientific experiments to occur on a scale of dramatic proportions such as the story of Frankenstein and other experimentation done with humans to distort their true biological make-up that violates the higher rules from above. We feel dissatisfied with who we are at times. We want to change or enhance what we are. That is fine and good. However, we should realize that there are repercussions to violating the human genome in a way that would be much more dangerous to us and our future existence than to any level of rebellion against those who breathed life into us in the first place. We are the masters of our own universe and they will allow us to destroy ourselves if our rebellion and anger is too high or if we choose to no longer exist. It is all placed back in our hands. We have access to the greater good at any moment we desire. The choices or decisions are our own a universal level. The masses control the way the reality occurs, and we can rewrite that reality with love, peace and harmony within our households and around our national borders. We can learn to love ourselves in all our imperfections of character, personality or physical bodies. Finding true peace from within will create a wealth of love and happiness that has been available to us all along. It is not on the outside of us but rather on the inside. Search for the answers from within and there you will find your direct connection to the truth and all wisdom that there is available to you to access.

Atlantis is still rising. It is rising within you. It is rising with sun in a dawning of a new day. They knew the truth of who we were and what we would become. They knew the origin of all things and the spark of God within all of us. They knew that we were masters of our world and there was now limit to *knowledge* as long as one chooses not to abuse the *knowledge*. We must not misuse *knowledge* to oppress others or harm the natural Earth or even the economic system of the Earth. *Knowledge* is available if we promise not to distort the genetics of humankind and allow the natural course of evolution to evolve like a beautiful flower opening to it's highest potential or a quasar of blaring white light beaming the purity and fullness of the human soul. *Knowledge* is available when we all work together in the brotherhood and sisterhood of all humankind as we search to find answers to world problems.

In our world today we have all the elements of ancient Atlantis. Our knowledge of genetics is almost at the same point of intelligence. The same goes for our knowledge of the Natural Sciences, Biology, Horticulture, Agriculture, Mathematics, Zoology, Chemistry, Technology, etc. We parallel their culture and could even evolve to understand the powers and secrets that lie within our Quantum space to harness the affects of new scientific laws that would allow us to integrate other abilities if we are entrusted to not violate that space as well. Much has been hidden from us there until we are ready and have resolved our simple human behaviors toward one another and the physical realm around us.

Here is a restoration of truth and life. We carry the truth within us to grant us the quality of life we desire. Let's rise into the knowledge of Atlantis without the mistakes that followed. They began with a very high consciousness and plummeted to a very low state of consciousness. We must rise again to be able to awaken to the things we had known in the past to reveal the light of our future. We, like Atlantis, must rise back up with the sun into the light of pure wisdom and a renewed positive outlook into our future.

Chapter Nineteen

Violets in The Grass

My thoughts became still and a long pause of awakening occurred in my mind. The dream or the journey had not come to a stop. I could no longer hear the stream of consciousness rolling like a river of ever flowing information The visions and dreams stopped momentarily as I rose up from my computer and stretched my arms and realized that the sun was shining so beautifully outside. Then I walked over to the door and stepped outside.

I walked along the grass barefooted and felt the green earth under my feet and took in the fresh air and sunshine. For a short moment I breathed in the smell of lilacs and lavender that was growing in my back yard. The natural beauty of all my garden drew me in like pure running water in a desert. I stood amongst the evergreens, lilacs and ornamental trees and then looked down at my bare feet to see the lawn had a large patch of wild violets where I stood. I kneeled down and reached out to pick a small bouquet to see if anything would happen. After all, the changeling never left me. I thought maybe it should to reveal who I really was. I gathered the violets and nothing happened. I didn't see a mist or feel anything more than what the natural earth had. Maybe this is it? I wonder if I am to remain this way. Is it possible that the mischief I thought was bad was possibly the connection I felt from the Earth instead. I could hear so many different birds singing in their own natural choir. It was amazing to hear so many types of chirps and whistles all taking their turn singing and finding a point to insert their own tune. It may have been ten different species or more. How beautiful it was to hear the sounds.

I strolled back through the garden of trees, shrubs and flowers and smiled. I felt alive with wonder at all the mysteries that the natural earth had and felt myself sinking again, falling in love with all that there was around me. I didn't need to search any further as I felt a completion of this journey. The wind gently brushed up against me as strands of hair fell in my face. The white sweater I wore reflected the purity I felt after previously having the feeling of past-life fall from grace. I surrendered and then felt uplifted.

Then I felt there may be yet another journey left within me...I thought for a moment and saw a smile rise up inside as I could see in my third eye the mischief of a leprechaun winking. "Silly me," I thought. "When will I ever grow up?" In a quick and unhesitant response I commented back to myself, "I hope never."

In that instant the mist began to form around my feet. What happened next is more than just a mystery. A new adventure unfolded before me with the death of my old life and a new life begins...

"So it goes."

Kurt Vonnegut